LANDINGS

• •

Anna-Nina G. Kovalenko

Order this book online at www.trafford.com
or email orders@trafford.com

Most Trafford titles are also available at major online book retailers.

Print information available on the last page.

ISBN: 978-1-4907-7871-6 (sc)
ISBN: 978-1-4907-7870-9 (hc)
ISBN: 978-1-4907-7872-3 (e)

Library of Congress Control Number: 2016918982

Trafford rev.   12/02/2016

 www.trafford.com
North America & international
toll-free: 1 888 232 4444 (USA & Canada)
fax: 812 355 4082

CONTENTS

"Life is thing bitter, though quite edible"

(Author)

FOREWORD
("Smart Doggie")

- …All night was rain… O, o, o, o…

Grandma has moved away from the window.

- Noh*… (*yes-Sib.) - confirmed her neighbor and bosom friend, woman sitting on the bench near the window. – Such rain better for a spring…

- …Wait until dry up a little…

It's my grandmother to my request to let me go for a walk.

- Noh… - confirmed her neighbor and bosom friend. – Hey, how old are you? Three? Huh, d'you know some poem?

I climb up on the stool. A bow on the top of my head holding a bundle of short hair, and therefore my head seems onion head. (I know it from photographs of those years.) I begin to recite, loud, with expression:

- Come on, doggie, black nose,

Let's, my brother, study!

Sit up straight, be smarter

On the side not to fall!

- What are you, Petya,

No desire.

I'm still a puppy

Jogging, walking, roll around

Let me, Petya darling!

(At that my knowledge of poetry ends. What is pardonable for the age of "three")

- Look at you! - "Darling" - mocks me appeared in the doorway of the parlor a grandmother's youngest daughter, my aunt, ruddy teenage girl. She is jealous of my grandmother - her mother, and she does not love me.

Her dislike of little concern to me, I just love these lines; I like to imagine myself as doggie - so plump, with black nose, droopy ears... I do not know that these lines are continued – Petya's wise warning:

- Ah, cute face, you goosey, what you realize:

As later, as worse, you will learn it later.

Desirable time to blissful ignorance!

I
....
UNIDENTIFIED FLYING OBJECTS

"Exhausted darkness lyed down
I choked, also being exhausted
The underwater world was quiet
Without veil appeared dawn
Free and light"

(I.Badanova)

New York, July 15, 1989

The airplane to Rome, according to the timetable, would leave at 8:10 PM.

I came to the airport between eight and nine. Francesco was not there, anywhere.

A black, black lady employee at Gate 29 apathetically repeated over and over:

- Non-passengers may not proceed further.

Looming a while in the TWA terminal I was going to leave but suddenly saw him entering. …The time of departure had been changed for 10:00 PM and he was going to inform me, called to warn, but in that time I left home already.

At parting, in the buffet we drank a bitter beer. Italian speech sounded all around, as if the whole TWA building was to set out on a journey to Rome.

Awkwardly lighting, and then forgetting a cigarette in the ash tray, "…he said to me:

- Only tell me – and I stay"

In reply, I, imagining how difficult, how troublesome it could be for him to return his already registered baggage, what kind of epithets I would receive from his parents in Italy, and also not daring to confess my extremely miserable financial situation; thinking a little bit, I drew a card: river, two lean little figures at the bank: "He" and "I". I draw an arrow "flow direction" and say one of the figures:

- Francesco, go with the flow...

In my arms is a present from his heart—an expensive Ferrari fountain pen. When he is walking to the gangway of his plane, I hold to my chest the pen and I speak, after him by broken voice, a single word:

- Francesco...

New York, July 21, 1989

Francesco flew away July 15th. I awaited his telephone call five entire days.

July twentieth, yesterday, wrote a letter to the Gallery in Tourin that belongs to his mother. I went with the letter to the mailbox—and changed my mind to drop. Returned back home and in detail recalled my writing: nothing dreadful. Left home again; dropped. What is done is done. Fell asleep quietly, knowing that he somewhere exists and understands everything. And he won't say anything like "You apparently wrote this drunk?", how once unwashed American Paul responded to my playful New Year's Eve greetings.

Francesco will never venture to do that, what is significant about him.

...Woke up to a phone call. Italy calling "collect". The husky distant voice spoke simple, uncommon words:

"I miss you."

"…I want to see you side by side all my life."

New York. August 11, 1989

On my birthday came to the park—brought myself, as a gift, to the flowers… A white-lilac rank, the lilies bloom along the fence.

Run for my camera, photographed. The photograph I'll send to him, write on the back:

"Francesco walked here."

New York. August, 1989

The distant sound of an airplane what flying somewhere, collides in my soul with the ancient pain of parting… He was wearing a dark red short-sleeved shirt; and I could be happy, if I'd said then "Stay". Indeed, someone somewhere shall be happy!

(Some times, long ago… **S**… But about that better do not remember… forget. Forgot… Almost forgot.)

New York September 2, 1989

Today is a Great Holiday: at morning, 10:30am Francesco called.

～

According to Hamlet

... As a child, when I heard the distant rumble of the aircraft in the sky, I, along with other kids, lifted up snotty nose, shouted in chorus after the flying silhouette:

- Eroplan, Eroplan,
Put me in your pocket
And the pocket is empty,
There cabbage will grow up,
And in cabbage's little worm,
What's about that little fist!

With last words we hoisted up the little fists, studded with little fissures, so-called "chickens", whereas "Eroplan," patiently bearing the verbal abuse, moved on.

Many years went by; very rarely do I recall this banter. But even now, when, conforming to the reflex of the deaf, I raise my eyes (and even without raising my eyes) at the boom of remote airplanes, I strongly recognize at the zenith those morose dark eyes which turned to the fatal Planet.

I see all over... In spring, in the forest, on a well-traveled path there strolls a female human individual smelling of cologne. The scalp of some murdered animal hangs from her neck by way of embellishment. The slender arm thoughtlessly reaches for a branch that grows imprudently low, and pulls it off.

— Mama! - It cries out, fractured, its darkened leaves drooping on the ground.

...And even your sacred traditions not more than painting colors on the pieces of dismembered wood.

"I see all over"

"Absurd, poor people"

~

The first letter from Francesco

I remember that icy night when even the stars were lifeless,
Looking up shivering, blood flowing the color of ice,
Hemispheres, galaxies I saw multitudes in gaping laughter
Of the infinite at all men
The Polar Star trembled white and strong,
And the other ones followed its strong suit—
This to me represented nothing good,
All this hectic fallings of white poles
But suddenly I saw a different one, lonely there

Dressed in a soft spring flower's blue light,
And in Her silence, in the mute expression of despair
It was all the dearest beloved to me.
Yes! How I loved that little lady-star' look,
So taciturn, small, her gestures and body motions,
Like the crossing of a heart is latent in her
To save from the wretchedness—
In the case of falling down
All men

~

January 5, 1990 Milano, Hotel Santomaso

Morning is not at all wiser than the evening* (*Despite Russian proverb: "Morning is wiser than Evening"- author's note). There is important, that a man (person) was wise. In that case he (she), in the morning, being rested, becomes wiser and makes mostly right decisions. But unwise ones - and I belong to their number - rest all their hopes upon the mornings as if upon an unseen, all-seeing provider whereas the morning is merely part of the circumference of the clock, arriving from somewhere "East" and departing to somewhere "West".

~

January 6, 1990, Milano, Hotel Santomaso

...To make from the diary pages inner soles—to escape the cold;

To cough hoarsely;

To re-count the coins, being afraid over-spending for a small cup of coffee;

To blow the nose – secretly - into a mitten (on the street)

And have a presentiment of a great happiness - are all things compatible.

∽

January 7, 1990. Milano, Hotel Santomaso

...Visited a Cathedral - one black guy from Senegal showed me the way for a thousand lire.

That merchant of glittering knickknacks turned out to be the only one at Piazza la Republika who speaks English.

On the notes, prepared for the Orchestra, I wrote:

"Santa Maria, save the life and the freedom of Ivan Demyanyuk and of all innocently condemned to Death."

This is my partisan's sacred wish.

Nunc et in hora mortis nostrae*(*Now and in hour of Death of ours—Lat.).

Amen.

Yet, it seems a communal telephone is vacant.

Morning of January 8, 1990.

The streets of Milano, especially those which are close to the Vokzal*(*railroad station), swarm with sexual maniacs.

To have your life in danger you do not have to wear décolleté or to be blonde; enough to be a woman and simply walk down the street.

∾

Milano, January 16, 1990

TO A LADY FRIEND, WHO DIED IN EXILE

My Dear Inna Moiseevna,

Inna

I write this letter in Milano, but to mail it to you (thou) to London I would do it only from New York.

And thus will be shorter way to the addressee, taking in account a labor enthusiasm of the Italian Postal-service. One and a half hours later the bus will come to take me, among the other passengers, to the airport. I am going to sit there all night and write to you, to thee *(*in Russian there're two forms of appealing to: "you"- official and "thou"- familiar). That is just the point, I am endlessly and hopelessly a provincial woman, therefore I venerate before intelligent people, before education, before erudition.

And yet for that reason it was so difficult for me until now to use "dear" with you.

Well, it's resolved. But forgive me please for "My Dear": in our Russian villages often even moms are called "Dear (Mother)", "Darling Mother"* (*"Matushka"). And I feel you a very relative, although urban.

For so long I did not hear anything from you. And without contact with you at present time it is impossible to survive.

Awful! It's freezing to the buttocks to sit on the cement steps (Oh, pardone! On the marble...), and the thick stratum of the stupid Italian press (for a thousand lire) does not save me from a cold... Could spend my final money for a hotel—do not want to, I hate it there... Will write to you, and be warmed that way.

Then, in Milano I was invited by a young man whom I saw five times before in New York. His mother (if she is really his mother) is the owner of a gallery in Tourin; her name is Isabelle Le Compt.

In New York she curated the "Art 54" exhibition where Francesco was gallery-sitting when I came in with my slides; the same young man who later invited me in Milano.

Our short meetings and talks, and those were five, mean to me a lot, in my wordless New York's life...

The first meeting

I showed him my slides. He advised me to leave them so his mother could look at them; and he made an appointment for my next visit.

The second meeting

I came to pick up my slides, and to hear his mother's opinion. Francesco was sitting alone, writing, how I guessed, a poem. We started to talk about Tsvetayeva, then about Hamlet. To his proposal, drink vodka (a bottle in the safe) I refused—this was hot weather. I invited them (his mother and him) to visit me for Okroshka*(* a Summer-soup). I left my slides there.

The third meeting

He came alone (without his mother). I did not ask why. We walked in the park... Were sitting on a green bench, talked about Hamlet... drank coffee, somewhere.

The fourth meeting

He called by phone and invited us—my daughter and me—to his Long Island house. I could not surmount a dull obstinacy of her (daughter's) transitional age, and thus, departed alone.

He was waiting for me on the end of the platform. Kissing with meeting, we swiftly knocked with each other by our sunglasses.

Inside the courtyard of the big house toiled, or managed, some men, introduced to me as workers.

However, they soon disappeared, noiselessly fled in their little truck...

Not one painting or picture was to be seen in that house; excepting a refrigerator, all the inside was empty.

I was swimming in the basin; the water there was cold and clear.

Walking down to the ocean' shore, I collected little white pebbles.

Francesco all that time was resting on the grass, with his face to the sky.

(Running past him with my little pebbles, I involuntarily noted the slightly strange expression of his face: as if he were fighting with a temptation unknown to me; however, wealth always adds to people - even though slightly - an oddity...)

Then we sat down together on the grass, read his a bit muddled poetry, drank bad coffee... and talked about Hamlet.

Fifth meeting - a parting

He called and asked and his question sounded a little inappropriate: if he might settle down near us; with me; with us?

Surprised, embarrassed, frightened at the disclosure of my poverty and ashamed of it, I answered: "This is not easy". Feeling myself something guilty; I promised to think about it a little.

On the edge of evening he called again, and told me: "am flying away."

There was time to go to JFK—to see, to see off (to stop?). I was on the verge, so was my money.

Between the meetings; Matrioshky

One day Francesco told me over the phone how he visited Moscow. He was five years old; up to that time he'd always lived in the Long Island house that belonged to him from first day of his birth—the house located on what is now the B.View. Near him constantly was his tutor, the neat Englishman Bruce.

Occasionally a thickset Spanish woman with a mop in her arms caught his eye as she went past him to the house; and disappeared after a cleaning job was finished. Somebody invisible and inaudible brought cleanliness and order, filling the refrigerator with food, the basin with water…

Such was all his childhood. From the courtyard he could stroll down to the ocean—the beach, of course, belonged to our hero too. A neighboring house, always empty, silently looked at boy by its deserted windows.

Only once, in one window of the aforementioned house, appeared a face of girl.

The face absentmindedly surveyed the green space with the boy Francesco in it, from time to time bringing to mouth and sipping from a cup some drink—probably tea or coffee. The coffee finished, the girl turned and went away forever—either inside the home, or away from the life of the residence.

For many long years following that occurrence, imagination of Francesco drew the ghosts, spirits, aliens, which descended once by special voyage to Long Island. His older brother lived in an identical residence at the C.Road, with his own tutor. The brothers did not love each other. Mother with her husband lived in Paris, father with his wife in Rome.

When Francesco was five, his father came and took him, temporarily, to Rome, where he lived, and then to Moscow, where he, a modest Italian millionaire Romano, planned to do one profitable contract, and pretty little boy Francesco with his presence could help or rather promote the measure's success.

Moscow streets of the 60s stuck in his memory: clean, lighted, lively. During the business and adult meetings Romano Jr most of all wanted to drink (he'd been thirsty), to pee-pee/wee-wee, to sleep, to ask, to touch, to pester...

Once, finding a free minute, father brought him to "Beriozka", the store where were so many beautiful things. But most of all, the dolls named "Matrioshky"*(*plural from "Matrioshka"-author's note) affected him with their beauty. Father bluntly refused to buy "these expensive and useless trifles": he was nervous, afraid "failing" somehow. Lost in contemplation of "Matrioshky," the kid did not notice how he lost sight of his father. He went out to the street (it is likely, Gorky St.) went to the right … went to the left; started to cry. People immediately surrounded him, asking him something in Russian. He did not understand and cried louder and louder. There came a policeman, also speaking that strange Russian…

That evening his father came to the Police station, reached by phone at the Hotel. Francesco for that moment gobbled ice cream and conversed in English with a red-haired guy who came to the police station expressly to contact "his young friend Francesco". Several days later both Romanos returned from Moscow: Senior to Rome; Junior—for many, many years—to Long Island, where he'd attended university and then travelled throughout Africa and Europe, writing poetry, and been bored.

"Matrioshky"—he never saw them anymore, unless in dreams - them, and also that girl, with a cup in her hands, behind the curtains…

In the late autumn of 1989, at his 30th birthday, to the address of Florence pensionat "Via del Serragli" a parcel will come from New York. He will open the white cardboard box: from a white like snow mat will gaze a funny black-browed "Matrioshka" face… after the First, the Second, and after the Second, the Third; after the Third… the Seventh, lowest in the hierarchy, holds a small blue note:

"Dear Francesco, happy birthday.

Matrioshky"

"God bless you for Life and Poetry,"—I thought, while plunging those wooden beauties into the cardboard box.

∾

He flew away. Then he wrote me letters. From everywhere: Rome, Tourin, Florence, Milano… Called collect: I paid those bills, became indebted, and was never able again to get out of debt.

Well we, he and I, had decided to see each other; however, it was not simple. I did not have money. No money all summer, neither all autumn. … In winter, one collector suddenly sent me a check for one my painting, which he bought from me more than a year ago… But I could not obtain a ticket for the end of December.

So, Christmas, we were apart, New Year' Eve - apart.

At last, I connected with a courier company, "Now Voyager". They stripped me for an extra fifty dollars for registration; a hundred more, as a "deposit". Plus, the original three hundred fifty—for a cheap ticket, which I did not receive into my hands, in the capacity of "courier", for two weeks in Milano, carrying some package.

I obtained a visa, which I was to receive within two days. Lady - Consul rendered to me such special condescension, taken in trust that I won't stay in Italy but will return to my daughter and paintings, gave me parting phrase:

- Only be careful there…

At evening on the eve of flight Francesco called, and offered to meet… in Paris. ("What an idiot," noted my daughter.) I began to explain to him that, first, people like me, "stateless", should await the entry-visa to Paris not for minutes, but for months; and, second, now was impossible to refuse from trip without unpleasant for a "courier" consequences.

"And, third," - I thought - "where to obtain such money from?" At all, our relationship more reminded a sports competition between a hare and a tortoise… He seemed persuaded: promised to meet me in Milano Airport.

Humming "la-la-la-la..." upon the music of Mozart, (Simfonia Concertante (K.364), Andante) I packed up in a satchel my belongings, prepared my portfolio to show in Milano' galleries and flew away.

~

I am familiar with flight
So are my wings with weariness.
Scissoring roof of the sky
In mega-physical efforts
To meta-physical dreamy age
I fly, enamoured ghost,
Spring alcoholic, fly on the edge,
When winter, exhausted, falls...

With dawn arrived in Milano, gave my courier packet to my contacter, but Francesco was not in the Airport.

Along with all the newly arrived I boarded a bus, which went to the Central Railroad Vokzal* (*a railroad station). Call Francesco - no one picks up the phone.

Stuck out in Vokzal untill evening—hungry, dirty, with a heaviest satchel. Russian publishers from New York bid me to mail from Milano to authors living in Europe, new issues of "Chernovik"* (*published in NY, late 80s, Almanac of contemporary Russian poetry), they thought that way could be cheaper. My situation was complicated because of my ignorance of the Italian language. At the end of the afternoon an

English-speaking passerby helped me: walked to the Information Bureau and at night I rented a room in the cheapest Hotel.

(To whom expects to be in Milano, and in the same situation: cheapest hotels are marked with five little stars, most expensive hotels - with one). Here I spent four nights, for which a hostess stripped off rent from me as for six nights, and with that kind (Milano's?) plunder I could not do anything: pay, says, that's all, in another case I won't give you your belongings. The room was cold, narrow - a vertical coffin, and that was named a "camera". I caught a cold, coughed agonizingly... phoned Francesco: heard in reply a busy signal.

Decided: his telephone was broken. Thought else: he probably could not resist temptation to go to Paris during his vacations (he told, he is working in a school as teacher of English). And I was coming to meet all trains from Paris, tempting the surrounding sexual maniacs, which the streets of Milano swarm with.

On January 8th - the end of all vacations - I set out to find him following the address on the envelope. That was, how it turned out, the expensive hotel out of town! There called up him from his room hundred fifty seven.

He came out, rejoiced at me.

And yet, anew I see his dear face with humid beautifully outlined lips: black-brown eyes (black pupils—on the full brown cornea; the strange expression of the impotent fight with an unknown to me temptation...)

We came inside of his "number".

There was something different from "camera": a light room with a door to the balcony; color TV, the luxurious library of poetry, the bicycle in the corner, and my "Matrioshky", all together side-by-side on the bookshelf. White telephone... Francesco took vodka from a little cupboard; to warm up from the frost. I took one gulp "for warm welcome" washed down with coffee. Pouring out coffee by cups, he threw there a few tiny pills - sugar substitutes, he said...

Giving him, at his command, all my money, I lost consciousness.

...Came to my senses on the bathroom floor in a puddle of brown vomit.

I drank the offered coffee and switched off again... ...Came to consciousness again—at this time on the bedroom floor, felt the pain from strokes on my head, on cheekbones, on breast, on pelvis, on legs... I had seen over me the frantic sadist eyes, the foam in his mouth' nooks... Clenching teeth, endured the strikes, I kept silent looking directly to his face.

...Came to senses, heard my own tearing cough. The life instinct told: avoid his coffee. Unnoticeably I splashed out the offered drink.

Surveyed: there comes evening (or morning?)

With switched electricity light everywhere restlessly tosses an insane type dressed in unfastened, flung-open robe, glittering with a huge stiff red "shlong" ("member"); nervously sorts out the books, things; sits down awhile near TV set - also, like electricity, unextinguished; for one second looks into over-painted faces of Italian screen-heroes and jumps up again, falls down on the edge of bed and quickly masturbates with help of his own hands, splashing out the warm stinky sperm on the floor or directly into my face, eyes, hair...takes from under bed the orange towel and masturbates again—at this time there falls to a towel's share... Goes away for the kitchen, prepares for himself the abominable mash from hot water, green peas, and unpeeled (though chopped) onion; non-stopping wagging by his tongue some incoherent baloney, at motion gobbles, gobbles, gobbles from the saucepan.

Then - stinks.

Stench...

My things are scattered all over the room. I see my almanacs overflowed with coffee. Telephone rings, he picks up the phone. I hear his sentimentally croaking Italian "ma-a-ma", and English "bitch".

—Ye-as, ma-a-ma, she is bitch, but I like it. (No doubt, they discuss about me. Is not it nice from their side...)

—Ma-a-ma!! But on earth I told you: I need money, cash. All over, ciao, ma-a-ma!

...A kick on my ear. I close my eyes, endure.

A cough betrays me. I'm in my sense. Recite to myself meditations. Sadly, timidly there a thought appeared: would I hold through... when?

Through jointed eyelids I see: passing hotel is flying, of the geometrically and spectrally divine beauty, UFO. Hovers over the window of bedroom number one hundred fifty seven; sends me in sign of consolation its soft yellow-rosy-(light) blue radiance.

...A stroke on the head. With all my last efforts restraining cough, not opening my eyes, I see: the room became empty. Only nearly one of walls, lighted up from the left window, there stands the table. On that table a huge glass vase, full of flowers: Lilies, many lilies. Towering over them, affable nods me by curly dreamy-colored little heads Siberian Scabiosa, Snyt-of-fields ... Kashka (Baby breath)... Poppies... Tulips, light blue, lilac-coloured... In their shadows, is hiding,

gloomily turns yellow Cicuta Virosa (venomous)…
Enter three women-shadows.

TRINITY

Oh that obtrusive image of PERFECTION
With eternally changing faces
For many years repeatedly appear to me
In my reality, and dreams
Forever lonely, three together
They crossed my way, carrying yokes with buckets
Or hurried, passed me, embracing triumphal portfolios,
Or, guarding, followed in city lights
In summer day led out to the path
From dark and scary forest,
Then picking up, they pulled me into car
Of soon-departing train
And from platform waved after me
By three re-laundered, three reweeped handkerchiefs
Obtrusive triple image of PERFECTION

…Grandma, long ago and calmly gone from Life
Earthly, now from threshold sends me signs of the
cross.

My Beauty Mother, who died soon after grandmother,
bequeathing me: a pillow with feather, one handful
of Siberian earth and one glance at sky* (*first one I

gave away to her neighbors, second was confiscated by custom officials; third I keep for myself), bended over me so low, that her long black braids tickle my face.

Understanding, which efforts worth for her coming to me, I do not ask her any thing. She pronounces herself the word, by light wind rustles through the space:

- Galls...

...Then else, dissolving, like cloud:

- Tenth century...

From these strange words (evidently, giving me some important information about my origin or, maybe, about place and time for our with her future meetings) calms down, goes away the pain in my nape and behind ear; now I can turn my head, to see thee, third ghost, standing near the vase with the flowers.

Oh, my dear friend, you my older by intellect sister, do not leave me alone! With a horror, I think about ... about... to tell properly, I forgot and cannot remember his name, remember only the fear before him.

Here he is, appears from the kitchen in his wild negligee.

You snatch from the bouquet one branch of Cicuta Virosa, and lift your arm against him. Transformed to the black reptile, cowardly and discontentedly hissing, he creeps away from the room.

- Do not worry… Somehow you'll meet in your life real Francesco…

You, probably, erred, implying "real friend"?

But is that right or not, I do not have time to clear up: now you disappear too, and the fine ship UFO behind the window flies away, dissolves in the sky. No more flowers on the table… Real Francesco, helping me stand up from the floor, telling:

- Bring yourself up in order! I will take you to pharmacy.

Hardly stepping with broken feet, I trudge to the mirror, in the bathroom: the face is blackish-blue, the lips are covered by grazes, behind the ear - the sticky wound…

- Take it!—he gives me dark sunglasses and we go out from the "number".

I walk staggering, and, shaken.

My look is terrible. The head buzzes. An administrator of duty sits in the hall, thrusted nose into reading. Walking past him, I unnoticeable for Francesco leave on the little barrier my travel passport.

Before we enter the pharmacy Francesco gives command:

- Cough!

The assignment is easy: I cough readily, without any command. Then I hear, how he tells to the old pharmacist: "Codeine."

Afterward we proceed to another pharmacy, and there I'm also coughing, while he buying codeine - for himself.

On the way back to the Hotel there is a store, where with accompaniment of my cough he buys (or steals) a bottle of vodka. Intercepting my quick imploring glance towards a lady cashier, he binds my arms behind the back, and in that pose we come back to the Hotel... And on the streets, because of hard frosts, in the cement flower pots blossomed with pearly brooches the hoarfrost... If I remain alive, I will write one day in my diary:

"No blooming more beautiful than a blossoming rime"

The administrator sits in the previous pose, my travel-document already lying beside the key from number one hundred fifty seven. Now I know: past him possible to carry dismembered corpses.

In the room: cold, restlessly, drearily; glows the light... TV... Francesco swallows his pills with vodka. In the pose of a "poor relative", I sit on the edge of the chair furtively look into window, thinking about the beauty of those snowy, flowers; about that bouquet on the table... I recalled with a shame that I presented for thee flowers only twice or thrice, buying thought more about a price rather than about a beauty.

I even do not know, for example, which flowers are thy (your) favorite . . .

Suddenly a breeze arose behind window, diamondly sparkled in sun, flown up, the snow-flakes.

Over the times, kilometers and winds,

Your caressing voice answers by rhymes...

- Well I'm gonna come to New York and *fuck* your daughter, - by the way, sipping his coffee, grins Francesco.

I keep silent. The insult and threat are conceived especially ominously because he - what I was, how it is said, convinced of - unable to the normal sexual act, neither with woman, nor with man.

Sometimes indeed, probably, there'd like to talk about something, even though with a victim.

…Saw once the blue tulips
An oddity, fairy tale, the overseas countries!
Like sky's depths, boats of light-blue,
Like messages from childhood, where miracles—any.
To buy them, saying truth, I did not dare,
But, seems to me, know, of whose arms is it work.
Prime flowerbeds, high grassed,
Ah, sad fairy-taler, with smile of sly!
Naïve and wise - such he is only one
Narrated he us, how lives a mandarin,
He gifted to us the world of everyday—bizarre,
Where Gerda and Kay, and wooden soldier
Where dollies, and a rat, Lapland's deer,
Canals and the rosy, northern day;
Clink the bluebells in the middle of branches
But in cage there sadly sits sad nightingale.
What for there ruin these blue tulips?
What for there confine them in deadlock's glasses?
'll forget; and remember suddenly by cloudy day
Let them eternally stand in my heart.
(Inna Badanova, "Blue Tulips", London-1988)

But here he dozes by a short dream, sleeps hooked on
the bed's edge, thrusted by his schlong in the orange
towel. I sneak up to the door, try to open - it would not
give.

Where are the keys I do not know, to search, moreover to search him, do not risk. Could be possible to come out at balcony... To come out and to shout:

- Help!

...To hear in reply the creak of the shut windows?

I approach the telephone, pick up the receiver. Do not know the code, and cannot at all, handle the local telephones. But what thou think? God-Foresight helps me, my daughter's voice answers from another side of the world. I report the address of Hotel, ask her to mail money. A mental sketch: the administrator, received money, goes up by elevator and knocks into door of the "number", but when the door opens, I slip outside and with money in my arms escape, run into direction of Airport, along the long corridor, hiding behind the everywhere growing backs of administrators-in-duty...

Francesco jumps, damns my cough. I put the telephone receiver down in place, had not managed to explain anything to my girl, and, in all probability, had evoken in her the chrestomathian reminiscences about the charming prodigal Mme Ranevskaya from the "Cherry-Orchard" by A. Chekhov.

He compells me to open my mouth, splashes in my throat some spray. "What is that?" "Cocaine," he jokes. (Jokes?) Mutters:

- You'll marry me… Tomorrow!!! No, today… Today as to be you Senora Romano.

I keep silent, or rather coughing. For him the unity of marriage seems the excess-precaution, but what about my remains, such flattering the title "Senora Romano" won't reserve to me any chances for justice.

- Where is your passport? Where is the passport?! - Meantime rages Senor Romano, rummaging in my satchel. His attention from there diverts to the television. On the screen the reportage from Romania: to people, right after Sir Chaushesku was murdered, there distribute bananas, for some reason from the West.

Close up a young woman, the Romanian woman with the baby on her arms, senile way bound up the kerchief on her head, with the pale and beautiful face of a movie star.

What is she talking about, easily possible to guess: hitherto, up to now (bearing in mind the murder of Chaushesku and bananas' arrival from the West) her life was awful.

Hearing her words, harmonic sound of her contralto-voice, or the codeine from my cough had effect on Francesco: his eyes are imbued with tears.

- I am a bad person, - sobs he. - I am a narcoman, thief and murderer. I am hopeless.

Godless is murderer's beginning:

That was in Africa... Some boy... Then, indeed, in Tourino... No-no, in Fiorenzo... He met in café a girl, the beautiful girl Laura, invited her to his Hotel... She wanted him he saw that, then, perceiving him as an ordinary impotent, behaved injudiciously, offended him by her laughter...

- You aren't jealous? – suddenly, timidly, even ingratiatingly asks me Francesco. - I was in that time so lonely...

As if awfully, I do not feel jealous. Well maybe, scarcely. Then if he had more time, he could dedicate to her an excellent poetry.

"Ma-a-ma" assisted to sweep up the wet traces: a ticket for airplane, a next-first rate Hotel, a new mission of enlightenment... The sons did not ripen yet for the big business.

- Hypnotize me again, - asks he, winding in the try to hug me. I wince. - Turn me again into the snake.

I can not hypnotize. And this, as a matter of fact, is not necessary.

❧

Continue to write already in the Airport building.

Yesterday morning (how turned out, for eighth day of the described meeting) he left for trot, dressed for that privileged business (exercise) the abominable dirty attire, remotely reminding sporting. He grasped up with him also the bicycle, up to now parked in the corner of room.

During their (his and his bicycle's) absence I gathered, how could, my things, dragged up my bag (satchel) to the door, threw upon my raincoat; and as soon as the room's door opened, letting them in,—I jumped outside and broke into run (at least, so seemed to me), hiding behind the back of, an accidentally found here, Chinese.

I came down to the administrator glued to his book behind the counter, and I, remember, said:

- I have to talk to you.

Near him, behind the counter, stood and automatically smiled a young Italian cow (heifer).

Feigned they do not understand English, they begun to respond by poking in my hands now the travel-passport; now some pills, calling these "medicine".

Arrived here one more general character of that Hotel, its owner, a brilliant green-eyed handsome man, who entrusted me, one after another, three his business cards, telling something in Italian - probably, inviting more than once visit their institution.

Of course, according to all the rules of that decent tone, I had to leave, and according to the rules of the simplest dynamics, limping on foot into direction of Malpenza* (*Airport in Milano) and doing about four or five kilometers per hour, for two days and two nights exactly to arrive to the departure of the airplane "Milano-New York".

But I did not want to part with them so, that finally two of them (first and second ones) began to speak English with a nice London accent.

Green-eyed Eduardo Brandolese took me into his little back room. Availed of the reader-on-duty's translation, I told (briefly, of course - to the point) about things, which were going on and could be going on with me more in their hotel.

According to the smiles in reply I guessed: they could not bewail me, and modestly could bury me at the expense Madame Isabelle Le Compt.

However, they called police.

Policemen rode a long while.

Brandolese all that time emitted the smiles, evidently understanding that his smiles suit with his face. (Yes, in that moment I, even by all my efforts could not equalize with him by attractiveness.)

To demonstrate what in my personality they could lose - here was nearly slapped to death not a fly but a human! An artist! - I opened to show them my portfolio with photographs of my artworks. Heard the polite, trite:

- Very nice.

Policemen arrived. Young, with faces plump, indifferent, so alike each other, that I do not remember exactly, were they whether two, or three, or four.

"Are you sure, that he - Romano - in his room? Over there is his key."

...And they left. To go upstairs did not bother. To help me to get to American Consulate, i.e. to transport, declined: said, that it would cost them much, you know they aren't Milano's police.

I persuaded to call to the Consulate: there everybody left already - that was on three o'clock post meridien. I talked with the officer on duty whose name was David. David advised me in my situation (meaning the absence of money) to stay in the Hotel, to rent the room and to await some help from New York. And he imparted to me that in reality, the Hotel owns a bus that rides to Milano for free.

They (hotel's staff) ordered a phone-call "collect" to New York, broadcasted to my daughter my request for mailing money, dictating the address of Milano Central Postamt* (*Post Office) - not their hotel's for some reason; gave the telephone receiver to me. I talked in Russian, but two words: "Sadist," "Onanist" are international, and the cashier girl-cow responded to these with soundless laughter, showing four times with eight-and-a-half wholesomest teeth. We, one can say, were going to become girl-friends, as well as I had a reason to think, looking at her:

"Sometimes it is the happiness to be fat."

The administrator - came running, put into my hands a fashion magazine. Flitted from the pages yellow, red, black, dock-tailed dresses for hire; hunted down looks of models-mannequins... Through a window glass, not copletely drawn by curtains, suddenly I saw coming out with the belongings from Hotel, Francesco.

I came to administrator and said:

- But I saw.

Whereas he pretended, he did not understand, and offered me to read an Italian newspaper. I repeated:

- But I saw, how Mister Romano was coming out from Hotel.

He answered: yes, yes, he came out.

At present their mercy quickly switched to the anger, and I simply do not imagine what could happen to me further, if there was not once more the God Foresight: in the back pocket of my jeans by miracle kept safe not taken away, crumpled a fifty thousands lire note, which solved the fate of my forthcoming night.

If thou could see, how brightened those responsible faces by appearance of that twisted in eight, almost mouldered note! Something similar could be grasped maybe only in the sole face of Raphael' Madonna, kneeling before the naked infant who thoughtlessly caught hold of her drapery's lap.

Listened to the end of their long solemn speech about such a favour was given to me, a ninety-thousand lire room on the eight floor for half the price, I set off for there to sleep. This room was as good as the one hundred fifty seven, but I did not feel any pleasure, how I did before.

Closed behind myself the door, inside, I realized, that was tired and in consequence of beatings and pills of "sugar-substitute" could not concentrate myself at anything. I was very frightened to stay forever in that shape: surely almost everything is possible to overcome, only if the mind is not lost.

...I did my first Milano's sketch - the view from the window.

At evening, I was called by phone to go downstairs; some generous official from Consulate (and maybe the Consul himself) sent two tickets for metro.

While my return into room upstairs the barkeeper called me and gave me toast and tea - stuck in my memory his thin face; dark, sad, all understanding eyes.

At morning, I came to Milano, to the Consulate. Passed, like the other ones, the austere Customs examination for presence, or rather, for absence of a bomb in my portfolio; came closer to the glassy barrier, and smiling blue-eyed official gentleman looked at me. He recognized me thanks to numerous autographs, which Francesco left on my face.

- Were you raped? - asked he with unintelligible to me voluptuousness, and the eyes of his, waiting for answer, were going to turn from blue to yellow.

People in line impatiently pushed me from behind. I coldly asked him for giving to me a suitable form.

At long last, this is not yet the court.

Looking past me, officially disappointed, he also coldly thanked me for an "attention to the criminal persons" and expressed regrets concerning the fact Consulate cannot help me anything, because meanwhile I am not an American citizen (to be citizens of U.S.A., emigrants await at least five years).

Nevertheless, he said, I could leave my "riport" (report) in the International (foreign) police. Gave me the address - how appeared, fake, false one.

But I, despite of all, I found this police: a huge, one-floor building, more resembling garage; and in front of that, waits for forms of "riports" a crowd of many thousands (and I do not exaggerate) - evidently, of nobody's citizens. When the crowd goes closer to the entrance into the police-garage, it's met by the group of bandits, dressed in police-and military uniforms; they drive away people back (that way a cattle could be driven away), they allow to cudgel, non-speaking any one word English, and at all any other language, except their own. I understood that there is stupid, senseless idea: to search a mystical end of line for mystical forms whilst I had to receive money from New York at somewhere Central Postamt; in Consulate refused to lend, did not give any cent, and that was because I was not their citizen.

I spat ouit (mentally), started by foot (presented two tokens for Metro ended) to search Postamt. Young Gipsy woman with a suckling on her arms catched on my raincoat' lap. I cried out, recoiled back, walked faster, hearing her pursuing steps, fervent whisper:

- Senora... Manjare* (*to eat)...

Walked, noting by my eyes everywhere the beauty of Gothic architectural forms. ...Thought: "Memorials of Yore."

Rising up my head, to the sculptures, saw the stony genitals; by subconscious I timidly drew a woody, Orthodox cross on the human grave; and crossed.

No Memorial of Yore higher (than that).

~

...At past night, in the room for fifty thousands lire note, *I saw dream about an ancient, half-ruined church. I was climbing by rotten wooden ladders rungs up, following after two priests dressed in black. I was wearing the long gown with floral design (I wear it now, I changed) on my shoulders was the red Russian shawl (it was left in New York).*

"...In the time of the ascent up towards right cupola the priests passed, easily came up by the wooden ladder." I lay on the platform between sky and earth, devoid of possibility to come down or go further up, following my priests in black.

My Dear Stormy Stream* (*translation of the name "Inna"), my Lady Seagull, then social security number such and such.

What for, with what illusory hopes, emigrating then from Russia, we flew to different directions?

...During farewell tea party, suddenly, behind the window, crashed down to the root, the old birch-tree.

Then there was a calm, spring weather.

Second, Tourino's Letter from Franchesco

I am in night restaurant
where of cynical, mocking eyes
The thousandfold salute,
And crockery's guttural sounds
Grows cold over back:
Really it will start to me that Hour?
Help. Fence me, God, from the zoo-
logical torment
In the alcoholic intoxication recall of the memory a
Home
-museum of Christian Love,
Triangle of face, the gaze browny grey
Monotonous showing of, water coloured, dull drawings
Dark red: Spas-na Krovi* (*the Savior on Blood-Russ)
Underclothes cross's rusty chain -
Like by all Old believers...
On the blood does not save. Her ghost better to leave,
Call up sole God to give for a pagan
Acres of desert
There is sand; howling of wind, dry grass rustles.

In the name of the Father... and Son... et Spititus
Santa...
Amen.

The letter from Fiorenza

Since I remember myself,
All the best happened today.
...Awoke of sparrows' family conversation behind the
window.
Automobiles, scqueaking, braked
Tip-up a calendar winked by historically a modest date
Came mailman – brought from you
Purifying charming snow.
I plodded on it by thirty years old,
A slightly mad poet,
Muttering all known Russian phrases:
"Dostoevsky... Raskolnikov ... Pushkin...
Chekhov... Tsvetaeva... Nina... Moskva..."
My heart wildly beat,
My dear, amore mia,
I wanted to see you side by side
I write from town of Dante
Since I remember myself
All the best happened today.

The last letter from Francesco

...Balance... It's an impossible, odd word
Early morning when you're drawing
The blue iron curtains of sky
To see how at all:
Like freckles, there cavities,
Torn holes...
Their monotonousness is more painful for eyes
Than the dazzling
To you, the inhabitant of the stony womb of New York,
Streets' darkness, stench appear by a synthetical skin,
Sinister mantia, hiding foul secrets
Then you would darkness fell on the world forever,
The world of New York City,
And that you could make a smoking wasteland
Of the whole synthetic and polluted mess
This vacuum of black, white and blue
With a coffin cover over beautiful corps of life
So Policemen are right in their avoiding of depressions,
The night is on duty for them,
And reliable for them its black constancy
(December, Milano)

∼

"...I love Nina she is like a bright ray enlightening my
world's darkness"

(the inscription on the almanac page, covered by spilled
coffee)

∽

The night

In the middle of the cold empty Malpenza airport, bothering by her own presence the quiet job of cleaners, there sits a thin, disheveled woman with a dark blue face designed with red polka dots, and writes, writes, writes...

If that was not a devotion to writing, she could be taken for a fallen down prostitute and driven out... Approaches an armed (not with knowledge though) type, asks to show her documents.

After the document was showed – he just shone forth: "Russian? Russian!" And, done, salutes, departs. In the travel-document, really, written "Ukrainian," but oh, he exultantly grasps about international connections.

∽

Extended over street
The laser-ray,
He's straight, but round shoulders
Burning and green
The trees long ago, out
Lost foliage,
Their green present
That ray to the Christmas.
He's there, over buildings,
Over life he streams,
Beneath by little lights

Variegates Oxford Street
To elements wholly devoted
And eternally alone,
What for to him a fashion,
Showcases' violence?
He aspires to peoples
He from over roofs' steeples,
Plucks and vexes,
Prickly and green.
(Inna Badanova, "Ray," London 1988)

Malpenza, morning of January 17, 1990

Dear Inna Moiseevna,

The rest of night passed in intercourse with people.

...At last night, descended from somewhere above, set down a while and calmed down in a distant, left (from me) corner of Airport's building, one young hippy from California, Roberto.

...Came in and asked me about something (at first, in Italian) a girl Marny from Michigan with her old dog - inevitable, faithful companion during their voyage, which was done through Europe.

We - all three of us - expected to fly in (and through) New York with different flights.

The Tale of Marny

My name is Marny,
I'm stone, I'm Iceland,
I'm girl named Marny,
I'm stony Iceland
From Michigan State
My father - I didn't know him,
About mother I remember:
Once stuck there
Two red cherry-berries
In the green lock of hair
I a long while collected
Some, any money:
I wanted to study,
Now I'm over thirty...
Listen to me, lady,
You, are an artist?
Can I that your newspaper
Put under my dog spread, a bed?
...When my ex-,
Then my cheating boyfriend
Leaving me, gave me
A puppy as consolation
Everybody was satisfied
Including that Horilla
Separator with her cat
Here we are, dog and I,
Deadly tired
To be on a visit in Europe
(To be on a wander through Europe)
Like crossword puzzles

To guess copliments' real meanings;
To ask any favour
From them, for my own
For by price of sweat and blood
Obtained bucks *
The treasury emptied,
The credit card
Get back, to our dusters,
I'm an artist too,
I'm an as-sanizator
A mermaid and a witch
I'm a stone, I'm Iceland,
I'm girl Marny
From Michigan State

(* money)

- You know, - said Roberto, - here they took me for a terrorist. Policemen. I casually fell asleep at the second floor, at the floor. Employees scattered, and policemen surrounded by circle and pointed on me their automatons. Until I woke up, stood and pointed. And all is because my satchel's fabric is with little flowers.

(His satchel's fabric was indeed with little flowers.)

- Satchel's fabric with little flowers... That is probably, the uniform of terrorists, - presupposed Marny.

- Oh, if all terrorists wore uniforms, - tore out from me.

Finished their job and sat down by us to the first morning bus into town two cleaners: one was Italian, the other Arab. The Italian aloud dreamed to marry some Russian - these are beautiful - and provide himself with fifteen (but better—with sixteen) kids. The taciturn Arab treated everybody, separating unto little lots, with delicious oranges. (The number of us was five, excluding the dog, but oranges' number was two.)

It is good to be with simple people.

After seeing them, we (Marny and I) decided to get some sleep: I - on chairs; she, did not forget to brush her teeth before sleep, on the floor, close by her dog. Her single pillow she had she ceded to me.

Appeared and soon flew away by first flight boys-students; they told at parting the story about how they taught a lesson to some haughty Frenches because "American nuts."

Flew away also a tender beautiful little girl Rebecca, pressing to her chest my sketch: "Is it I? Is it exactly I, not boy?" re-asked she, as did not find on the sketch her pony tail. And her parents pulled and jerked her at her hand.

For Marny there begin bustles with dispatch of her dog, dying from tiredness. A voice calls me to the ticket-window number ten to entrust a packet for New York's employees of "Now Voyager" - you know, I fly as a courier...

Goldenhaired Roberto is going to the boarding. His flight is two hours earlier than mine. Nearly going away, he suddenly abruptly turns back, runs to me, quickly presses to his chest, and kisses - in eyes of surprised audience which crowded around the booking window number ten.

To him, to them, to thee, I - ready to cry like Gorky's Mother* (*Heroine of M.Gorky novel "Mother") - send my unspoken innermost, burning:

- Dear ones...

〜

Now they all already flew away, whereas I still sit...

Now fly up...

Fly...

There no blossoms more beautiful than a blossoming rime.

January 1990.

II
....

SUMMER AND WOOD

"...Fools! Make me whole again that weighty pearls
The queen of Egypt melted, and I'll say
That ye may love in spite of beaver hats"
(John Keats, "And what is love? It's a doll dressed up")

January, 2002 . . .

Do you know... That is to say, you know, of course, what does mean "commivoyageur". I do also know. For the first time, I remember, I came across this word in a book-collection of dramas by Tennesy Williams: there's a heroine of his "Summer and Smoke" Alma, after multiple and many-years-standing, unsuccessful tries to deserve a love of her childhood' friend, John, in the end, I mean, of that drama, accepts from hands of some unknown "Touring Commivoyageur" a pill from headache, which (the headache) tortured her so much (can you ask why?!), and she follows him, that unknown Touring Commivoyageur, closely, to his hotel.

In "Russian Dictionary", published by "Berkley Books", I found such interpretation to the "Commivoyageur":

"commercial traveller", or: "commercial pilgrim"

By the way, has someone met on the streets of New York (City) a tall handsome man (could be wearing glasses) with a travelling pouch over right shoulder (pouch's straps could be tattered), dressed in intercepted around waist by belt a raincoat of marsh color? (Generally speaking, on me that color could be called "olive") If you ask him about something, for example, how to get West Houston Street, he might answer by sobbing voice, in meantime forming his mouth into a little hole, which tempts you to fasten an invisible button - such is his mouth's design: "buttonhole". He smells something tasty: white wine; common onion (little bit); female perfume (little-little bit)..

That is Michael, and he is the commivoyageur.

Michael, Michael… First, a pair of light eyes from behind circled glasses, aimed to me from his starry height. A timid (and sobbing, as I already noted) voice:

- I do not want to be intruder in your life, but... Would
you be indulgent enough to have a cup of coffee with me?

I, crushed by such polite, carried over to ceremonial,
appeal to my personage:

- Sure!

Michael, Michael... Telephone rings by Sundays,
twelve thirty afternoon of New York time: complaints
to his unbearable and interminable loneliness-es
(pl.!), which are so understandable by - especially
Russian— - ladies/artists . . .

Remember, the other day I heard by TV news about a
car accident in Kansas City, what took away half-dosen
lives. Anxious from that bad news I could not sleep well
all night, and early morning of following day called
to Kansas, I called, myself: if he's alive or...? A cruel,
barking woman's voice responded:

- Michael? What for! What f *** you need! Who are
  you!

I:

- Oh, sorry, wrong number...

However, felt relief, gladness: alive! In that woman'
voice was no grief.

Michael, Michael... Here he is, i.e. his ring, twelve thirty.

- Ah, Michael! I was so worried for you; but, your wife soothed me...

- Wife!? Which wife? What woman? You, probably, dialed wrong number.

- No, Michael, she said clearly: "This is a Michael O'Neill's residence."

- Aah.... Namesake. No-no, it's impossible, yet my phone, my cell-phone, is personal property... Well then, I had only to be absent to toilet... Let's forget it. I love you. I shouldn't say so ("Why?"), but my lips betrayed my heart. I love you.

Michael's coming to New York, our trip to restaurant on West Eleventh. Beautiful moments: in front of him fried chicken; in front of me pasta sprinkled with cheese. Holding in right hand a goblet with unfinished "Chardonnay" Michael stares at photography on the wall, over a head of a laughable waitress: black-white cityscape, in particular an arche-entrance into a (urban) courtyard... Replique - his comment or evaluation:

- I'll come back again here. I LIKE THIS.

(She laughs.)

On the way back from restaurant - a little theater; he examines by eyes a repertoire over a shoulder of some lady in checkered hat smoking near the wall; and he says to me:

- Someday, at next my coming, we'll go to see the theatre.

Our parting in train's car: he has to go out before me, his hotel is here; apolozies for non-inviting:

- I have to wake up tomorrow early-early, then to fly...

Three more days after: going back home very late at night, entering in train's car, I stumble upon... Michael, who coquettishly curved his torso over sitting beside a nice blonde in a black beret, clasping by his right hand to his chest the tattered strap of his travelling pouch, while his left hand squeezed a light-brown paper bag, which appetizingly smelled by fried potato "French Fries" and inexpensive, still warm American regular coffee:

- *...I do not want to be intruder in your life, but . . . Would you be indulgent enough to...*

Here I touch his shoulder:

- Michael! Good evening, Michael!

In response - frightened eyes color of the seas unpolluted wave. And here are his last words:

- Ah… But my flight was postponed because of company suddenly fired a new employee and now I'll fly tomorrow early morning all right my stop to go out that was nice… to ride in the same car…

- Yes, yes, - manly I kept up a conversation, - same to me, nice… in the same car… Especially as to different directions…

Train stopped. Train started. He waved by free hand from platform.

Such he stuck in my memory. The blonde in black beret obtained from her black coat's pocket a little packing of two pills, "Tylenol", from headache. I thought then:

"For some commivoyageurs is not necessary to leave New York."

Since then he does not call me; vainly to wait by Sundays at time twelve thirty. A gnashing of automobile… Anti-fire siren… Barking of some stray dog… What does it matter, anything, except of his dear, slightly snotty voice.

February

Meanwhile an exposition of Salon des Independants in Paris gets closer.

Six months since I corresponded with Yoko, my Japanese friend-collegue by the Salon. She, like me, skipped expositions for last six-seven years, because of financial troubles. But now, we decided, and we wrote each other: we'll take part, we'll come to Paris, and we'll see each other on the opening! Her last letter ended with a phrase:

"Maybe, if we all together…"

…Last meeting with Michael, with that tasty smelling by coffee and "French Fries"… the little light-brown bag…

What am I going to submit to Salon? Could be good if "Russian Field," but… "Russian Field" was sent to Michael while my attack of compassion. That happened before my contact with the barking voice. (Wife?) Agonizingly I wanted to see him, even if by one eye; to fly to Kansas, to pass by his windows. I saw that dream: I flew to Kansas to pass by his windows, and what I see is: the entrance to his palace-residence blocked by disgusting and nacked sixteen breasted sculptural baba *(*married peasant woman - coll. or dial. Russ.), produced by Mikhail (Michael, in other words!) Shemiakin; the sculpture usually, in reality, blocks the entrance of SoHo's Gallery "Mimi Fertz" (perhaps, that's even Mimi):

- Who are you! What f*** you need here!

(Such nightmare…)

March

I hold in my hand the old letter from him, to be more precisely, a postcard with an Effigy of Jeanne d'Arc, the card was enclosed in envelope, and contained a written on its backside:

"Stranger who trusts, who shares… Thank you, NIna!" Respond to my "Russian Field". "Stranger" - that is him (I told you!) Although… Jeanne d'Arc on the post-card looks horrible, looks like a robot, in her (?) uncomfortable equipment, with her (…) waist tied, and hair short, smooth, like TV hostess Joahn Rivers. Only without J.Rivers' charm, though.

April

What am I going to submit to Salon?!

In each walking along the N.Y.C. streets man with bag over his right shoulder (without bag too) I track down dearest features. Another day I followed (stalked!) walking through Thirty Fourth Street a man in intercepted-waist-by-belt a raincoat of the marshy colour, which (raincoat), during his walking, fluttered like a sail. To catch up, to pass, and to look into his eyes! - Outstripping was uneasy, I caught up only when that man stopped to wait the sign "Walk!" - blessing to cross Eight Avenue. I looked into his eyes - recoiled: eyes were not light-green, but dark-, and hair—not curly, but...

(I did not take in account the factor: back of Michael's head has a special form, such a little saucepan; otherwise I did not run in vain, just because of the colour of the raincoat...) I trudged back to North-West; came to Central Park, sat down on a rock; jogged along, passing by me, harnessed in strolling carriages horses, and on each coachman's seat there is undercovered michael.

May

Surely he forgot me? I have to paint, to do painting, but no inspiration.

I am in class of ASL, Art Students League of New York, where soon a bell will ring, and artists would be allowed to their easels, up to nine forty five post meridiem. Monitor Michael (again, Michael!) moves tables, chairs, easels with such noise, so inaccurately, that last Monday I already had temptation to ask him, outvoicing that, created by him, noise:

- Are you deaf?

But I keep silent, today is Friday, and all this hellish noise is illustration to my condition-decision:

"NO LOVE." ("Love does not exist.")

Already June

"Life—this is a chain (line) of sufferings, interrupted (from time to time) by joys (small ones)."

With such conclusion I walk passing by blind walls of Lower Manhattan, along which ones, I see, timidly creeping shoots of uncultivated plants, more offen of Morning Glory, flowering frequently with white, rarely with blue.

And I think improvising: what if someone (perhaps, Michael!) secretly admires us, i.e. Morning Glory and me, hiding behind stony protuberances of Lower Manhattan? Tears away! Yes, yes, let us all think this way: someone secretly admires us.

Still June...

I might ride, walk, following after him not only to Kansas, but much farther, to the edge of... But he did not call me there, and to all my hints he responded streamlined:

"Day will come..."

That respond, and that post-card... Those post-cards... All that stuff was pathetically scary. Though what am I going to submit to Salon?

Might be possible... Ah, yes, I sent that too, I gave to Michael: he is also an art collector from whom I received in respond the regular post-card as appreciation, the card with image of... of whom, you think? - Jeanne d'Arc in military, uncomfortable equipment, with hair a la Joahn Rivers. He what, storages loads of them? A writing on the back side announced:

"Be kind for everyone you meet is fights a great battle." (Philo of Alexandria)

Imagine his great battle with a multibreasted wife for possession by cell-phone... In the heat of the battle my neighbor by easel from left asked me to do not hit canvas by brush so violently, because it bothers him.

"Sorry."

Further I have to control my gestures.

"Summer and Smoke" This is my favorite thing by Tennessee Williams, this is, maybe, a sole thing by Tennessee Williams, in which, i.e. where, the author, failing himself, does not kill Woman, does not burn down her alive, does not drag her barefoot and in red robe into Lunatic Assylum, but, instead, he crosses Woman's life road with a touring commivoyageur. That happened to me... How that happened? ...Sat down on the bench. Then here is an imposing, cultural, grown-up man... in raincoat of marshy color...

Compassionly asked if he could be helpful, here's a pill, i.e. a coffee...

What, pain inside? But, however, alive! Search and believe, Alma. Pain - inside. Horizontal composition, big, the biggest from all I painted before. (Except "Marina Tsvetaeva," what I left years ago in Moscow.) My neighbour by easel from left, that one, after finishing his still life with corn (dried corn) cobs, gives me all paint leftovers from his palette. In an overturned and confined space-cloister, near dark wall - a woman-ghost in blue, with a cigarette* (*not with a pill: pills do not smoke, moreover do not blaze) in her arm: Smoke.

Summer season, prices for tickets are astronomical, hence the ticket I bought one way, relying to the Russian-Ukrainian "avos"* (*maybe-Rus.), i.e. "perhaps, some one will buy the painting". In the centre of that composition space are rocks-beds, two of them. Slightly behind the Woman, who combines in herself the features of the blonde in black beret, and mine, plus little bit(s) of someone else (someone else's), from the ceiling, grows down a weed: blue flower of Morning Glory: Summer. Let it be a hope.

From time to time, for anatomical correctness, I look at mirror, this way posing to myself through tears: Smoke.

Rose called by phone, Brazilian, my colleague by New York co-op Gallery, and she is also a member of Salon, by the way, by my protégée. She almost got ready to go to Paris, but changed her mind: why to go, if there's a chance to fetch her artwork by me, with me? Summer season yet, those tickets are so expensive - logically. She brought her rolled artwork to me to the Gallery.

Now I am just obliged to fly, it turned so: Rose told clearly:

"DO NOT DISAPPOINT **ME**."

I am packing, took from the stretchers also "Summer and Smoke".

Sunday Twelve thirty... One o'clock... One thirty... Two... Three... How to heal my soul trauma? Once I read in Almanac of Russian Writers Club (of N.Y.) a story by young female author, the story's title, seems to me, "Telephone". There one girl, abandoned and forgotten by her boyfriend, vainly waits for a phone ring from him. To reduce her soul tension, she turns over the pages of her diary, and she finds in that diary, forgotten records of futile waitings close to phone.

I found by green cover my diary for past years. Well... Here is, recorded by red ink, with out a date:

"V. - man, does take shower (does he take at all?), just twice in week. Such a person can not be a husband, lover, and so on..."

(Who is that "V."? This is not I am looking for.)

"...For breakfast has eaten..."

Oh, this does not connect with the telephone theme. Forward!

"S..."

S...

"...November, 18. Cold inside and outside... I am for some reasons only in socks. Man, whom I feel a soul mate. Skinny, dark blond... He kisses me as an omen of parting, "See you". Leaves... I jump out, outside, to catch, to tell... Run over snow. Feel: one sock fell down, from my right foot... From left foot – too... Woke up..."

- Ah, that was a dream. Further, forward:

"...In cafeteria took coffee; when set down behind the table, Joe, sitting next table, surrounded by ladies, slapped on my hip, meanwhile smiling so sneeringly that I understood: this is not him, but his seventy thousands per year slapped on my hip..."

- Forward...

"...January, 3. Downstairs, after class (i.e. after painting class) went to the same direction - we are neighbours by lockers - with my longtime, noticeable weakened, idol..."

That was the skinny, dark blond man, whom I liked so many years! I used to come to cafeteria in certain hours, when he used to sit here behind the round table, by window, and I used to come to look at him...

Oh, that was He, whom I saw in that my dream! O'kay, further...

"...He said by his back:

- So early (leaving)?

- Yes, well, yes . . .

—Good for you . . .

Snot! I.e., furtively darting a glance at his formerly gorgeous profile, I saw the long, transparent snot, flowing down from his nose's tip, possible from his right nostril. Recoiled, moving off, I squeezed out myself squeaky:

- Good night . . ."

Hm... For all that, we should never delay with declaration of love.

∽

June 11, Tuesday

Airplane arrived at morning, which was a deep night in New York.

Chilling cold... Now I stepped in a bus to city direction; sat closer to a driver, who could not take his eyes from own reflection in mirror. My neighbor by seat - a sharp profile, fair fluffy hair - gave a voice, complained at cold. I looked at him again, once more: light cotton shirt with short sleeves; light pants; sandals over bare feet. By flushing movement I obtained from my bag a pair of socks. He dressed on, felt better, warmer.

The artist-nonconformist Paolo Mucciarelly, the son of Francesco ("Francesco... ") Mucciarelly and Mirka Dal Angelo, how I understood from a given to me catalogue, was on the way back from Africa, where he made an installation. Paolo helped me, carrying my cart, to get to the place of Salon' exposition Espace Auteuil what was located on the far West of Paris. And then, cowering from morning cold (my extra-sweater was too small to him), continued his way home, to his native Italian town "Breccia" (according to that catalogue also). I stood for while, waiting.

Since no one living soul came here - the hours of artworks acceptation did not come - I started wandering around through neighbourhood Espace Auteuil. Jetlag affected me, I wanted to sleep. Moored to a closest cafe-bar, left by entrance my cart with belongings and paintings, Rose's and mine. Came in...

People in cafe drank coffee and drank beer, nervously and greedily smoked, meantime staring at the screen of TV-set hanged in honored cornerlike an icon. There showed a football game, played France and someone else. About France participation I did not know, but guessed by deafening screams, yellings of monsieurs and madames with mugs and cigarettes in hands and in teeth... Came inside a big, very big and very pretty girl with bright dark eyes... Something at her seemed "transvestite" or how it's pronounced/spelled. She sat behind a table in front of me, then swiftly turned back and asked me in French, if she did not block the screen image. I hurried to reassure her by gestures: "Oh, no, no, no," - hardly controlling indications of my happiness and appreciations: yet, before her landing I needed to heel to left, towards a blue column, to hide myself completely from that "Screen Image".

And came in yet another habitue de cafe, a slender gorgeous brunet ... Kissed someone, pressed hand to someone; set down near that dark-eyed girl; glanced at screen...

Noticed me, lop-sided holding a tiny cup with bitter coffee for 4 and 1/2 Euro... Moved to my table... Started talk in French... in English... I gave him invitation to the opening, gave to him and to another table-mate, smoking like locomotive an aged skinny madame, as a symbol of equality of genders I gave to her. She, inhaled her cigarette, moved with invitation to the bar counter, and here my new table-mate offered himself to me as a model - nude, of course. I said to him: "Unfortunately, I have no studio in Paris." (One may think I do have it in New York.) Then he asked my telephone number; in respond I asked him his telephone number. He, "Jean" ("For you I am just Jean, ha-ha-ha." "But what, for someone else you are Pierre (Michele)?" "Ha-ha-ha…"), did not give me, because, he said, he "moves somewhere". Yet I gave him a telephone number of Salon, let him phone, especially whereas he won't phone.

The match finished by French defeat. Everybody here mooed and howled…

The girl-transvestite snatched out from her jacket's bosom a microphone, and this way turned out a journalist, she began interview the men in the bar. Here she is: took all her interviews, and left. I was leaving right after her, rolled my cart towards Espace Auteuil followed through the window by mocking glances of Jean: "Hey, you, artists…" ("Hey, you, commi…")

Such commi-, I mean people, leave in you an inferiority complex: you aren't right, not their species.

Aute…. opened, participants crowded and arrived. I took out the canvases, untied sticks-stretchers. Rose's canvas stretched easyly; her work's title"Euro": a table, on that table a pink flower in a vase; leaves-snakes hang down and climb down from the vase over the table, and on surface of the table-cloth, plus everywhere to look - "Euros," coins, bills, all in "Euro". This painting like other Rose's works, voluptuos by color (for someones by contents as well). But my canvas because of long being in too tight tube (transported that way) wrinkled, and so now, to smooth, I watered it from back side of image, carrying water from toilet crane by scanty portions in plastic bag and in my mouth. Two old fellows, he and she, offered me help, actually, awfully bothering: in concord by four hands stretched canvas following some their own system, which did not work out; muttered, scribbled the stretchers by pencil, crooked-bended my canvas, smoked and dropped or just shaked off an ash on my poor painting.

Now I see a woman whose face seems familiar by... cafeteria? Ah, yes, she is from Secretariat! She said she'll bring from her home at day of opening a black ribbon, to fill these gaps, i.e. fields-shields, which appeared after re-stretching on the edges of my painting. Yes, she repeated after thought, she'll bring and fill.

During a next voyage to the toilet I saw a small table in the corner, there a hillock of sandwiches; I took one with cheese, ate.

Whereas my stretching operation approached to the end (my helpers, distracted on something more absorbing, deserted me already), entered in corridor a smart blonde lady; introduced herself: "New President of Salon."* (*Franky Tac - 2002 and further); then immediately moved away. Her hard, laconic answers to questions & appeals deprived of any illusions type of: "maybe if we all together".

Jury: company of elders (how time runs, oh Lord!) settled down to seats behind the tables, which were brought to them. Someone's solicitous hands spreaded out in front of them those sandwiches - o-o-o-ops! Those were, how it turned out, for jury! Well. The jury's ruminating, chewing. Here also brought to jury drinks: waters, juices. Washing down... Ate, drank, backed, filled, and now they give out membership cards. Gave the cards to me also, Rose's and mine, garbling everything: names, dates, genres, occasions. To say in all honesty, my gender, I mean sex, i.e. my feminine race, in spite of all was still for them identifiable...

Artworks are given out. Yoko is not in sight anywhere: probably, she could not come, could not overcome, yet in Japan is also summer, thus, also high prices. She, like Rose, in shortage of recklessness, i.e. abnormality (what's in plenty of mine). Although... In her letters she asked repeatedly about Romadin (Moscow artist – oh, also Michael! Such epidemy...) Asked to say "hello" to him, without taking in account some remoteness between Moscow and New York. But neither Mr Romadin nor his whitish girlfriend "Du" (such pseudonym -alias, strange, right? However, short), who could not drive him away from Yoko unless by words: "Let's go from here don't you miss buyers" - they are not in sight.

Here is an English-speaking sculptor, my neighbour by area of packing/unpacking (now - of unpacking solely). I found him to ask: where, by his opinion, ("by your opinion, Sir...") possible to get a cheap place to stay: hotel, etc.

He:

- You are what, from Moon?

I:

- No, from New York.

He:

- What exactly "cheap"? I just today go back to England, and I won't be here at opening.

- Sorry. ("Pardon".)

I felt to faint.

More and more the difference on times affected me: in New York was midday, time to sleep, bearing in mind the night before without sleep. I searched by eyes, and did not find, one more protégée of mine, Clara C., yet she lives now not far away, in town Grass, or, rather, near town Grass, what is near Nice... By a telephone card which I bought in newspapers kiosk I rang, she rejoiced in, sounded happy:

- Oh, come here! Fetch me the catalogue!

Turned out, she dispatched her artworks (watercolors) to Salon by special delivery.

Loaded with tied to my cart catalogues - such heavy! - Stones, rather than catalogues. We'll remember for a long time our New President! - I rush to the Gare de Lion (Rail-road Station).

However, my train, last one for today, left already. Rush to the Gare Austerlitz. Two hours left before departure. Fighting with fainting, I do sketches by my weakening hand. Pass by and sit to their trains normal women - normal, yes, tick asses and with their husbands; I drew one of those: with a roughly painted face ("mascara"); she steps like a duck, a forward, attacking player of her timid brood. I am looking around in search of sign of some "free medical emergency help" for case of fainting. Do not find, however.

Absence of help is a normal.

Breakfast at Veranda I drink coffee, while she eats cheese, cutting by slices the loaf placed near her, cutting and departing into her mouth by scroogy portions; and I know what she's going to say after chewing this little slice:

"I need to rest"

Then she'll swallow, stand up, take from next to her chair a little doggie Lily, put it into her armpit, and waddling, she'll direct towards her rest/bedroom...

- I need to rest.

(!)

On half-way to her rest/bedroom imposant Clara with curly Lily-in-armpit suddenly brakes to say:

- Today, at six thirty p.m., my sister Rachel comes to me, and she is going to spend here for a half-hour, while her doggie is going to be in Hair Salon not far from here, for haircut. And I want you to sing for us Russian folklore songs, Rachel loves that.

She went to hers. I, after washing dishes, hurry to my little fligel for pencils and paper to draw from nature the flowers of her estate: poppies, jasmine, wild onion/garlic... I'll name the last picture "Cape d'Ail", "Garlic's Bay".

Six thirty:

Vot mchitsia troika pochtovaya
*Po Volge-matushke zimoi**

(*Yet, races the post-chaise troika

Along Volga-Mother by winter)

...Ah, barin, barin, dobryi barin,
Uzh skoro god kak Ia lublu,
A nechrist-starosta-tatarin
Menia zhurit, a ia terplu*

(*Ah Master, Master, kind Master,

Soon'll be a year since I love,
But unbeliever, headman-tartar
Reproves me, and I endure)

"Nechrist-starosta-tatarin" for me associated with Clara, with her treatment of her servants: yesterday she yelled, again, at her gardener, probably, thinking that way to increase a harvest in her garden; while she, without understanding Russian, takes this (that, the) song for a some reason as a "Lullaby".

Rachel leaves: time for her to leave. I put plates on the table, for dinner-for-two. Clara asks me to show, i.e. to explain how to operate with her new computer.

June 16. Sunday. Breakfast on Veranda

Clara, sitting down, says, that I cannot think about being here, i.e. in her house, to the end of show:

- You cannot think about being in my house to the end of show, six more days; four days already passed.

("Oh, yes, oh yes, for tomorrow you already invited-allured a single art dealer who should not see me in company of you, Old hag.")

- Oh, Clara, I just was going to tell you (relax!), that today – today is Sunday - I am leaving to Nice, from where I am not going back: there is Russian Orthodox Church…

- Ah, Russian Orthodox Church. In Russian Orthodox Church might be new Russians, wealthy people. I want to sell my property, my ville. Take with you photographs of my ville, show them. Help me to sell, I will pay you commissions. Not much, though…

("But you lie. For packing up your things in New York you, Clara, paid me by pair of old socks… which I threw away immediately after. So, did you pick-up that?")

~

By the sleepers of abandoned rail-road I go, roll the cart towards Grass, towards a stop of bus to Nice remembering my dream of past night. *In that dream I found a crushed pigeon, i.e. dove, I even myself, accidentally, stepped down on it, then picked up, to throw out from the way; nevertheless, seemed to me, it had some signs of life, some tries to move, and thus, I began to carry it in my hands; carried, did not throw away… Now, nothing to water - I bended, tried to revive the dove by my saliva, he (it) reacted, he (it) were coming to life! And I already carried it (him) like a pet animal, like my own home pet, like someone whom I could and should care for...*

June, 19. Wednesday

"Dear Rose!

I got your e-mail letter soon after I reached Nice and found Internet Cafe, brothers Italians run it. An access to computer is so expensive! I only scarcely read your e-mail for my sum, then I will (I do) answer by regular mail. Clara C., you remember her by New York, has a new computer, at the beginning I stayed with her, and by her request I searched for her in net the right art dealers, also teaching her simplest procedures; however, she did not let me to check my e-mail: she was afraid I might "change the secret code", can you believe that? Well then, and now I occupy a room in Nice's pension*(*boarding-house), the room is vacant while its tenant, Gabor (full name's Gabriel, possible, "Gabor" because in his, Gabriel' veins, Magyar blood flows) is absent, for seasonal construction works out of town. I met him, and two more Russian guys, Sasha - street musician (earns money for his mother and sister who live in Belorussia, while he himself for economy sleeps at nights under a bridge), and Marat (speaks French very well, therefore found here a job, the job of colporteur—pedlar) in a courtyard of Russian Church.

I went out after service; in the yard sat down on a bench, then I hear: next to me people speak Russian. I dared to ask them something.—I got into conversation with them... The guys showed me a house, where Russian writer Chekhov dwelled (or stayed). We saw an exhibition of Niki de Saint Phalle* (*Summer-2002 Niki de St Phalle organized her retrospective show - gift to Nice. Those were last days of her life) Exposition in our Salon is ending, at Monday I have to pick up our works. Bye-, someone knocks the door, must be Marat brought me bread..."

∼

June, 24 Monday Nice-Paris

Behind the windows a lavish nature of Provence: mountains, stones, woods, flowers. Hope, our train would come at the proper time, thus I'll succeed to come to Salon before 4p.m., otherwise, how it was written (originally in French) in papers, "...artworks would pass into property of..." - not of authors.

I groped in my bag... oh, bread, and paper napkins: the filial, partisan concern from Gabor.

Yesterday, after Church service, I was introduced to his fellow countrywoman, charming Valentina. Three of us went uphill the mountain to the grave of Herzen.* (*Russian writer, founder of literature magazine "Kolokol", i.e. "Bell" 1800s). His bronze sculpture-gravestone turned green, but roses by his pedestal were fresh. Then we were walking Valentina to the bus station, to the bus to Monte Carlo, where in its neighbourhood she's working as a babysitter, but we did not want to say good-bye each other so soon, and thus, we three turned to a beach, were splashed under Moon to the midnight; later, after supper with red wine (oops, a dawn...) fell asleep: guests on the sofa, host—on the floor...

A girl from a neighbouring sit was detained, arrested by inspector: rode by train without a ticket. Similar things might happen to me, if he (inspector) came in car two stops later: my ticket is not exactly to the Paris: school of clochard*(*tramp, hobo) economy. This car is for smokers. Cashier, who sold me the ninety-six dollars ticket for one-hundred-six, asked: "Do you smoke?" I energetically shaked by my head: "Non pas!" ("No!") And then he gave me the ticket exactly to this car, car for smokers.

I arrived in time, succeeded. Societarians*(*perverted: "Societaries" - "Members"-Fr.) tittle-tattled near entrance, nobody paid a special attention to me: so-so, some shadow came. "What do you need?" "To take my artworks" "A-a, go and look." One thought very slightly comforted me: maybe, in the same way, apathetically, unconcernedly, neutrally, one hundred thirteen years ago, and possible the same ones, asked Teo Van Gog: "Who are you what you need?" "Here I am, came to pick up my brother's work."

"Aa, go and look."* (*Salon des Independants grounded in 1884. In following, ~1889 Salon exhibition, Vincent Van Gog participated.) My work, "Summer & Smoke" stood in Section B-31 "Surrealism", leaned to the wall. Instead of promised black ribbon - to fill the gaps of the edges - only fields of emptiness. Rose's painting I found in Section "European Art". - I did not know that Brazil is part of Europe. Oh, though, the point is... that "Euro!" (I wanted to cry again.)

- Sign of receiving.

I signed.

...En route.

By my way to Gare Austerlitz jumped from somewhere some unattractive gentleman in blue shirt, jumped and offered me to show the way to the Gare, did not get rid of me. By our way, after introduction speech about friendship between Russians and Americans, or between Putin and Bush (listening to him, I had to bend a little down, because my narrator was short, and I unwittingly recalled and regretted about Michael, such tall and gorgeous, and abandoned me like... like... Our friendship with him...), - outline of autobiographical story about his losing job in some "News", some "Press" ("Alright he's little shorter than I! But then, comforta...") and now wants to eat: "Appetite comes every day, is not it true, madame?" I, meanwhile, descending by steps into courtyard of Gare, regretted, that understood his French. He asked money straightly, I fumbled in my jacket's pocket for 2E, two Euros - it's not too little? - took out, gave to him, and he disappeared, though maybe ascended, rised: vainly I was searching for him by my eyes, splitting, riding my head following those leading upstairs steps. French... Pari... Parisian cadger! Neither his name, nor "thank you", i.e. "merci" was told to me. And I! With him! ...I almost cheated Michael with him...

June, 26. Wednesday

"Dear Rose!

I received your e-mail message after returning back to Nice, with artworks, allas! —nobody was pleased to buy them. ...News from you, about the gentleman who interested purchase my "Little Mermaid" for me seems a resque straw. But that straw, actually, little too weak: I worked over the "Little Mermaid" a whole year, in horrible conditions, in the corner of class, near a garbage can, where I was thrusted in by the discourteous monitor-misogynist, plus russophobe. But I did. And now: two hundreds... Wouldn't that man to add the price, a little, what if about fifty dollars plus? You know, I have to pay comission to the (NY) Gallery, and as a result, I am...

I am in shortage of money for a ticket back."

I saw a dream: *I shuffle by a shallow water of a clear river. See below: swimming, passing by, fishes. In my hands - the very dove/pigeon, which is my pet animal, and I am looking for a suitable tree on the bank, to land my bird. Here is the tree, once I saw and drew the same in Luxembu...*

Heart-rending howlings accompanied with automobile' alarms woke me up: "Princess Diana?" Someone crashed! With a sinking heart I moved towards a window: sidle, sidle... By only one eye: near a next door bar group of people stare at a displayed outside TV-screen. Fans! I have to get accustomed to... In the corner - rolled up into two tubes our (Rose's and mine) masterpieces; in the same place my "local" drawings and watercolors, altogether fourteen, could be sixteen, but two of them Clara C. took, silently put aside for herself then.

A regular cockroach walked by the wall. How good it could be to buy sleepers.

∾

June 30. Sunday Early morning

"Dear Rose.

Have some news from that gentleman?

You know what, Rose, as soon as you receive this letter, call me, please, to leave a message, to my New York "voice mail" service; it would not cost you too much $$, and I found here telephone booths in some "bar" where I can check my messages for a half of Euro…"

My glance at a bedside table: two books; one book with black cover, another with green. Gabor. However he knocked about the world, many things lost in wanderings, but Gospel and Prayer book kept safe.

"…About the man, whose room I occupy: physical education (PE) teacher, came from Ukraine to enter in legionaries, but was not accepted, evidently he seemed to them not enough impersonal…"

He turned to be not enough impersonal: "To them, you know, are wanted thoughtlessly obedient ones, indifferent to where, where to, whom, what to serve." He was grieved. Though, he was not only one rejected.

And they gave money, for a ticket to Marseille, plus food supply, a ration.

In Marseille he was walking along a pier, he looked at marinas, those sea views; dreamed to pass through to one of moored there ships, and go with it, on it, out to sea.

However, money was coming and came to the end, the food was expiring. He found a bycicle, repaired, and went to Paris. For while habited, i.e. slept in Bois de

Boulone, i.e. Boulone's Wood; cooked light dinners on "kerosinka"*(*oil-stove) what he also found…

Then moved to South: in Nice's vicinity; in Monaco; then one more place "Cape d'Ail" found shelters for nights: abandoned caves, abandoned houses… For some period he lived in a house-tower, abandoned sometimes, long times ago. Entry to that tower was possible for him only under a cover of darkness: do not attract people's attention.

Once a friend, his fellow countryman, came to and joined to him, now they were two. However, soon turned to be out, the guy used to urinate from balcony, and could not otherwise. It became uncomfortable. Neighbours noticed. There was necessary to change their lodging. That friend invented: during daytimes to go all around passing houses, which seem empty, and to mark those houses by yellow scotch: if next day the scotch toren off - somebody dwells in the house, if not – not…

~

…I asked an oncoming young guy "how to go out to Cathedral of Jeanne D'Arc," accompanying my question by a gesture of my index finger into map.

From his answer, also accompanied by gestures, I understood: two blocks up, then right: there I would see white-white "domes" ("houses"?), "ou coupoles" ("or cupolas?")

White, white cupolas... By wide stony steps entrance into Church.

She - her sculptured image: a flowing dress; from white whether a mafory or a women's cap, maybe kerchief - locks of brown hair; face of pleasing beauty, blue eyes' radiance... Suddenly and eerie thought: "And... She... burnt down!" Put a candle, hurry to exit, chocked with tears go round a clergyman, who already came out into passage, how I understood, to meet and to hear out timid raptures of parishioners-tourists, then to kiss them out... On the porch I dried my face: eyes, nose... On the same porch, from right, left all my cash-in-hand for poors and orphaneds, knowing, sensing: Jeanne will convey to them... Continued my way along the street of white-stoned buildings...

And here is a tree what looks like one I saw many years ago, first, in my childhood, in my Far Eastern village, in a distant corner of our neglected garden, on the border with forest. Then, in Paris (I came to participate in Salon's exhibition, also), in Luxemburg Garden (Jardin de Luxembourg): I was sitting on the bench, drew. When dusk came, a policeman approached to my bench and said: "Fermer!" That ment: "closed, we close". And I left. Recently that tree was recalled-seen in my dream there I wanted to land at it the pet-animal.

Sleep-walking I entered a glazed doorway; somnambulisticly read last names on mail boxes: "..." "..." "..." "Romano-Dietrich" "..." "..." "..." ...

Fumbled in my bag a card, for text:

"Dear Francesco!

Fate took me to Nice.

And I want - so many years later! - may you, forgive me all what was wrong, and I forgave you all long ago.

Nina"

(My New York voice-mail)

Thrusted the written down into a little slit of the mail box "Romano-Dietrich."

Somnambulist I went out. That's it. Today I have Mail-Sunday. Let forgive to Michael also, let give to him ABSOLUTION: he felt how he could (feel), he is in search, in reconnaissance raid... For completeness, for plentitude of feeling connection with the world, I might also... to my daughter, in Colorado. Though, she won't answer anyway, and I used to that. ...Imagine surprise of the owners of that mail-box, from the street - I turned back - "Rue de docteur…" OK, "Street of Doctor…" "…Docteur…" Forgot.

Tuesday, July 9 (JULY!)

Gabor brings each weekend from out-of-town, modest wild flowers, and I continue drawing; in kiosk what's in front of Art Museum, where's the posthumous, how it turned out, exhibition of Niki de St Phalle, I bought a cheapest aquarelle, for schoolchildren, all in all only six colors, but I am so glad to have it. Here's my finished naturmort: standing on a window-sill, a bouquet, in a glass jar. View from window: trees blossom by flags. The regular (was?) anniversary (of liberation?) in Nice. However, I like their touching consideration for their own history and their town's history

Morning, early one Thursday July (JULY!), 11th

Oh, finally, the telephone snack-bar-booth across the rail-road station, open.

I checked messages, they are two. First one - from my roommate Carmen, a bank teller in N.Y She decided to warn that I should not take from my account by small portions (I took by $20 bills), but better, she said, to take a big sum at once, for all these foreign bank services take for each operation, no matter what's the sum, by three dollars. The warning came I'm afraid too late. Actually, I have nothing more to take from my account.

Another message - from Rose: she orders to bring to her from France, besides a catalogue... condensed milk. Yes, that message ends in such a way: "I love French condensed milk", accompanied by smacking her lips.

(Squelchy sounds.)

Enough! - I hanged the phone. About "Mermaid" or, rather, about that gentleman, who's interested to buy - not any word. And once I had a true, veritable friend, Inna. The Kingdom of Heaven... "For peace from Heaven and Salvation of souls of ours, Lord..." "Lord! Where are Thou? What to do?" Lonely, deserted, worthless, long and inconsolably I sobbed between damp and blind walls of churches of Old Nice.

Later in the evening I recalled, how in the afternoon Marat dropped in to take me into Russian Library. There were two sweet librarians, Tania and Zoya (!), or Zoya Alexandrovna - Princess O., though she's Princess for her husband, and she is not arrogant as that "nee" (inborn) Princess O., who sells candles in Church, and who pushed off my invitation to the Salon exhibition:"We do not do commerce"; but, on the whole, the inborn Frenchwoman Zoya Alexandrovna learned and knows Russian language and good manners. She introduced me to readers, offered to select something to read. I selected Breshko-Breshkovsky's.

People sitting behind the table readers - on the whole of newspapers - moved, we sat closer. One hazel-eyed girl Tania (also Tania, like one of the librarians!) by last name Chaika*(*means in Russian "Sea Gull") presented to me a little postcard with image of Saint Vladimir, and with hers, Tania Chaika's good wishes to me. It's odd! What, I am returning to the Moon? At the head of that table some attractive blonde with impressive décolleté, sat and wrote; then suddenly put away her writing and hoisted a noise, i.e. started speaking inadmissibly for reading room, loudly: someone took away something in big portions from her New Russian husband; in principle, she spoke nonsense, and holded forth until Prince M. (in the beginning of her speech he noticed from the opposite end of table, that he'd "live not so bad," in evidence of that he picked up his shirt and clapped himself by bulky belly) offered her "to continue discussion in a some another place". And they two moved away, withdrew, disappeared to somewhere, I did not pay attention where to, how, when…

Then again, Ashran, a member of a new Afgan Government, reduced number of readers by one simple question:

- Who wants a beer?

I kept up a conversation over the table with an Armenian sculptor named "Gag Andrvik" who is forced, how he said, to lead a life of clochard)*(*tramp, hobo) after "a failure" (more probably, "a fraud", i.e. being deceived) in his last German Gallery. Not having means of subsistence and, then, a studio, he makes his miniature wooden sculptures in a square, i.e. in a small public garden. He demonstrated those to us, laid over the table; under his exponates he put reviews and articles from German newspapers and magazines for past years.

On the outside, in a small courtyard of Library, under some elder tree: chechens-refugees from those wars; their land, seems, already bleeding from shootings and bombings... They read aloud to their kids, fairy-tales of... Pushkin*(*Great Russian poet) Eyes of children... Within them, despite of all, were Trust and Faith.

And then I, grown-up person, became ashamed for my morning weakness—for that crying between damp walls of Old Nice.

July 14, Sunday

Gabor came from his out-of-town, asked:

- Well, are you ready?

A week ago he invited me to go with him "up" i.e. to ascend to one mountain in Monaco, he called it "Dog's Head" while I called it "Lying Profile". Yet, now it's for both of us "The Everest, which is important to subjugate". I drew that mountain before, from a territory of Principality, Grimaldies residency. ...Gabor looked at my attire: sleeveless tigh-fitting black gown and, also black, suede shoes on high hills – and he whistled:

- You what, gathered to Monte Carlo?*(*meaning a gambling resort, attracting prostitutes as well) But evening is not yet... Though... (Looked one more time) you are suitable for...

Soon the gown was replaced by jeans and tee-shirt, but shoes, since his white running shoes were too large for me, even over double socks - we left alone, i.e. on my feet.

Set off. It was early morning. From bus windows we saw sea-shore, now jade; now azure... Greenery of forests, buildings-ruins...

- There's a cave, see? - Gabor pointed. - Look carefully, there's an insignificant, plain terasse, I lived there. Rats got on my nerves, still remember. And the-e-ere, that tower, I told you already about. We lived there...

- Oh, yes. And what has become of your friend?

- A-ah... We met guys-clochards from Moldovia, encamped together with them; and that system of my friend worked so well... There is: yellow scotch not toren off - the house is ours. Came in: empty. On the table in a hall somebodies' documents, we thought: people died. In a kitchen cooked a meal; laid our meal on the table. With candle light sat down to have supper. Suddenly, door opened, and... Owner came in. He got rooted to the ground! Can you imagine? We also got rooted to the ground! Then the guys began to explain the situation, and he let us stay for night. Next day, following my opinion, my advice actually, guys clubbed together and bought paintings, brushes, and so on, and started repairing the house from inside, well, as to thanks. The owner, after saw it, let us stay longer, even paid for our works, and precisely that one - he's exellent worker, "techie", Jack of all trades - stayed with him, with owner, constantly.

- Ah . . .?

- I think his room's balcony exits to the yard.

- Aah . . .

... Arrived ...Quiet streets of Monaco. A quiet street...

- Now I'll show you one house where I lived. There is it, entrance, the door. But our "entrance" would be from a yard.

...Waiting, when someone walking by streets will pass us. ...Did. ...Begin to descend by steps of a slope to the yard. Down, down... (Far below the sea—the shore is visible.) Turned to the right - a wall with windows, and a little balcony of the level of... meters... about two-three-+ meters; a nail in the wall; a piece of a cable... Gabor starts climbing first, to give me hand from balcony. Minutes later I also, with stripped off and bleeding elbow join him on balcony. Now we entered into a small room, what served him formerly as an abode: a tidily inserted bed, on the shelf in head of bed - books, poems of Pushkin; paper icon of God Mother...

In the corner of room are reserves of water, in gallons.

But the rest of house space - concentrations of garbage, rubbish, trash, burnt pieces of furniture, and other things.

- Here even electricity is, I found then, look.

After some sorcery with wiring, found in the wall:

- Here lights up. Well, you always oppressed by being in big cities, and in New York too. You may come here to live for while; only one living here has to be careful, i.e. invisible and inhearable.

- But... ("But how about rats? For all that I am not ready to it.") Oh yes, I also dreamed for myself, when climbed to balcony: how good to use to come everyday out and to sketch each morning: this sea view, for example, such beautiful from balcony!!

- God forbid!! Morning/day! From balcony! If someone would see you - that's all, that's finish to you sketches! Here once at morning children climbed to me; I was shaving, and suddenly, see in mirror: their giggling mugs. You know, those hooliganic kids... But at that time there were kids... However, let's continue our conversation on the road. Forward, to this - how did you name it?

- Everest.

- Right. Today we'll subdue Everest. "Communists, forward!" - That is how said one, worshiped by me, Poet* (*A. Mezhirov, Russian poet.) I jump from balcony first.

∾

The subdual was not easy. Recalling our ascent, first of all I admire, admire and thank that Humanity, who paved along the steepness of stony terraces, along thorns, along boulders - a narrow, but path.

When the ascent approached to the end, my guide decided to shorten a way to the peak - to move onto rupture, i.e. onto nylon net which covered perpendicular parts of the cliff, for protection the mountain foot from falling down stones. And here

I - am I not idiot! - moved after him, professional sportsman… My left shoe fell down; further; noises of collapsed stones.

Suddenly, on a distance about five-six meters from standing on a ledge Gabor ready to give me his hand, I, hanging on my weakening and cut by net (+ . . .) arms, realized:

"I can not anymore"

Clearly, dready imagined my END, inevitable, horrible, painful end: a fall: I"ll rock - no escape - down, striking sharp protuberances, down, down…

And I might, I could fall, rock down, if that tree did not appear, lowering its strong, firm branches-snags down, towards me. By inhuman efforts I grasped the branch-snag, and yet… Gabor pulls me out last centimeters, on to the ledge area:

- No, look, for all that you such a great fellow!

He climbed down - I turned away in grip of acrophobia - took my hanged at slope shoe; I put it on, now is better; further… Strengthless I stand - my guide near me, and ruines of some low barrier masonry - on the peak of Everest.

- Look - Gabor says - no, you only look, you what, afraid of height? ("Yes, I am afraid…") Do not be afraid, here is the barrier, almost always is a barrier, come closer: such a beauty is below!

I looked down. Observed the world below, all these caves with rats, poor pansions-pensions with cock roaches, houses with yellow scotches and without-, gaming houses, and museums, churches, deserted towers, seemed from above cosy miniature swallows nests on the background of soft greenery of forests-hills and extended afar, afar, absorbed by space the water azure...

And burdens and risk of that ascend made sense.

...Moved into depths of "Dog's Head." To Gabor this place was already known: ruines, abandoned plum orchards.

- And now - he said – we may rest. Rest, pick up, you may put things here. (Dropped on the ground his anorak)

...Sat, swallowed plums: red and yellow, sweet and sour... Gabor confessed, that abandoned orchards - his favorite artistic image, maybe, he said, because he grew-up with his grandmother in a small Ukrainian village:

- My childhood is a land of abandoned orchards.

"Strange, but mine too" - I thought - "althought I grew-up at Far East, not in Ukraine, but also: a land of abandoned orchards. Or, more likely, neglected..."

But I did not say aloud, did not want to destroy the whole fascination of our dining-table on the grass under plum tree.

Went back; I limped because of broken shoe heel; Gabor cheered up:

- Well, you are such a great fellow! Before you one comrade, Dzhigit*!(*horseman, brave man-Caucas., sleng) went with me, you may know him, mountain-dweller, and looks like a person in good health, but, you know, turned sour on the half way, complained at tiredness.

By the entrance of pansion a young couple awaited for us: how it turned out, Valentina with her... son, Volodya.

- Why weren't you in Church?

- Well, we went to Everest...

- Whe-e-e-ere-e?

- To "Dog's Head", this is such a mountain...

- The mountain?! Why you did not take me with you? - Valentina leaped up. Gabor:

- No, you look, such women came!

After dinner with tea, wild plums and a lard (brought by Volodya from Ukraine) men departed, how we (Femmes) understood, to the reception center for Volodya to legionnaries, while Valentina and I stayed to wait their operation's end, repairing my broken shoe heel and taking in order the room.

∾

July 15, Monday

Telephone booth opened. I have two messages. First one from my roommate Carmen: troubles at her work (hit by chair into her head), depression: "I need your presence… your flat jokes ("Flat?"); your badly cooked coffee ("Badly? Well, wait, I'll make for you coffee…"); one word – YOU, your optimism…"

In conclusion: "I deposited at your account two hundred dollars, I do not have more, hope it's going to speed your coming back, I'll wait for you, I'll meet, please, inform me, please. Please!"

Second message from my daughter: "Mom, I called to New York, your roommate said you are in France. How is the show? Why are you stuck? For any case, I put at your account two hundred fifty bucks*(*dollars-sl.), could not put more. Poka.* (*bye- -Rus.)"

- Poka. (Ashamed. "And I, about girls… I have to… buy a scent-bottle, buy a flask of perfume…")

And I went into direction of a street bankomat.

~

Tuesday, July 16

"Dear Gavrusha!

(It's alright, that I call you Gavrusha? Mama and Grandma named so, when recalling, my father.)

Today evening I am flying to New York, the company "British Airways" sold me a cheap ticket, via London. The keys I will give to Marat, he would come as usually, to fill refrigerator by food; but if he won't, then I'll give to your acquaintance Arab who is on duty in a neighbouring bar. Then you say to Marat thanks from me for everything. And for his unselfish help to Clara C. with buyers to her villa, also.

I know you would not accept, even conversation about money… Here I translated for you into Russian two American country songs, which you love especially: "Hotel California" and this, "Baby" ("New Kid in Town").

~

(He does not know about my big surprise for him: I sent to his beloved Poet, Mezhirov, to Portland, "SASE" - Self-Addressed Stamped Envelope, precisely enclosed in envelope a post-card with a view of "Dog's Head" and with his, Gabor' address; I'd requested Mr Mezhirov just to sign his autograph on the card, and to drop it in a mail-box. Hope, he (M.) will sign...)

~

"...I have not enough words to fully express my appreciations for sheltering, for concern, and for Beauty of the world, discovered to me anew.

P.S To the airport will drive me my ex-friend, whom I lost and now found... Francesco."

~

In agency, for a cheapest ticket via London, they named a price in dollars: four hundred fifty eight, and plus forty eight cents. I overturned everything, my purse, turned outside my pockets: shortage... to buy that ticket, in shortage of four dollars and one cent. Well that one cent they could remit. But rest...

I asked the agent to wait for me, keep the ticket... ...Came out on the street. To search Gabor's dwelling? To take a seat on the porch of Notre Dame near that beautiful, tubercular girl-beggar? African guys spreaded out on the ground multitude sunglasses for sale. Here is a dog, stray, scraggy, dirty.

Suddenly:

Poi, garmonika, viuge nazlo,
Zaplutavshee schastie zovi,
Mne v holodnoy zemlianke teplo
Ot tvoey negasimoy lubvi!*
(*Sing, harmonica, despite snow-storm,
Strayed happiness, be welcomed guest,
Even being in frozen dug-out
I feel warm from unquenchable love!)

(Russian song "Zemlianka", i.e. "Dug-out")

- Sasha!

Put away his accordion:

- Such a lousy summer! Nobody interested anymore in Russian songs. Yesterday, for whole day only seven dollars...

And he gave me all seven, despite my tries to decline: "Why seven, I am in shortage only four..."

- Take, take, you are in for this... New York.

Next morning, for leftovers of coins, I went to check my messages, "na pososhok".*(*Russ.—"one for the road")

Messages were two.

1, first message from Rose: "I am in love":

"Remember, I sent you e-mail? And so, that was the same guy! He is such a... And such a great lover! (Smacking sounds.) Last night we had dinner, in a Restaurant..." (Name of restaurant, and address, details followed: what he said, what she said, what he said, what she... etc.)

"...OK, in sequence: in the beginning, in the very beginning, he said:

- *I do not want to be intruder in your life, but would you be indulgent eno...*"

2, next (message):

A husky voice - and came a sweet breath of lilies (perhaps, perfume for my girls in my bag), and I heard a remote sound of a passing by, in sky, airplane:

"Nina... A telephone call woke me up, that was ex-girlfriend of my father, she lives (and he lived once also) in Nice: she came back from Germany after visiting her relatives, and she found in her mail-box your post-card, then she called me immediately, I live in Vence, now I drive out from Vence, and I am going to wait for you until you'll come, home number... Street of Docteur..."

But here my coins finished, and I hurried to the street... -?

...On the corner, left from the glazen door of entrance, I saw: skinny figure ("How much he grew thin, oh my Lord! ...And grew bold"):

- You... So many years I wanted to see you. How did you find me? This house?

- By tree.

- What tree?

A long, long time we tried to find that tree, but in vain: not near home, nor around grew any tree, nothing grew at all, except sprouts of Night Beauty, plus uncultivated Morning Glory.

- Strange.

- Strange. Strange things happened to me too.

- Tell me.

- Well... That was a long, long time ago...

❧

I think that was a long time ago,
That year when I was in Rome
I entered into that city as always alone,

Serving life sentence of loneliness
Dragging with me as a luggage
The horror of my unattractive past
Wild thoughts possessed my head,
About the beauty which rejected me,
About Universe
With Its repetitions of resurrections and reincarnations,
Many, many thoughts, I can't express them all,
And then... Came in sight to me, this human world
Please, do not misinterpret me
I was holding it on my palm, it was mine,
Just mine, not some one's else,
Do I look like one who's worshipping
Some flat image
Like some photo from a family album?
Lord! Lead me out, Merciful,
From such displaying of greyness!
But rather there were sunny days,
The colonnades of quiet villas,
And my colorful desires, stretched out like shadows
Along empty streets,
Along silent stones,
Along the cool echoing corridors of museums,
Or the parched grass by aqueducts.
I would soak my taned face in a fontain,
Play insane games with Baroque fasades,
And with all my home-made brand of mysticism
Laugh aloud in the blinding light of noon
"Saluti, Vita!"

I walked through swarming avenues of breathless
nights
With only volume of darling Keats as my guide,
Through enlivening mornings of capuccino joys,
With only myself for company
And everything of nothing,
Until finally from cafes, or out of cheap hotels
I might observe the world playing games with my head
And happily thinking, that this is a mirage,
And that is also mirage,
Product of my weak mind, of a sick,
And spend another eternity,
I sank into a long-awaited dream.

(Free re-telling of Francesco's story, "An Incommunicado
in the Eternal City")

~

And now London Airport

Waiting for boarding to plane to New York

I am sitting on the bench, drawing the apple, what
Francesco gave to me for journey. Just now he must
be back to Vence and sits already on the meeting of
Anonymous Alcoholics, the course of important
treatment.

"Apple from orchard", - that's how he said. Then why
on its side this label, "Apple # 97174?"

From the beginning I drew by blue pen, then I found red one, and the apple on that drawing obtains a natural colour. Close to me - children's attraction, of two floors, i.e. two levels, with round windows. There cry, laugh, and play children of different races and ages. Here, three black ones: two sisters and a brother; barefoot girl-crumb, vawes by palm to her parents...

Approached to the counter, I mean to the counter of attendant, a fat Jew, wearing Jewish dress: black hat, black coat; with peys, beard, and other things. With him a boy about eleven-twelve year old, also fat, with "peysy". The father turned to direction shown by attendant. Came out... Here his boy frisky jumped inside of a hole-tonnel on the lower level, bursted out guffawing, and soon I saw in the window of second floor/level him, i,e. the piece of his striped shirt, and else, lively black eyes... He jumped out holding a photocamera - found? - gave it to the attendant, and continues to romp.

Kids, at first scared by dimensions and temps of their new mate, now they regained consciousness, they play all together. Attraction unites.

"Dear Gavrusha..."

Recalled:

"Docteur du Bois!" *

(*Bois - wood, tree -Fr.)

III

· ·

PARIS - CITY OF LOVE

Summer 2009

"...Where you in a hurry,
Seller of pies?
Where you in a hurry -
Lyon or to Paris?"

I meditate, or rather chant to myself these French children's rhymes - it's not referring to some of the world trade in pies, like Baroness N. Vodianova, and others like her, but doing my own packing to Paris with watercolors for exhibition (and per sale!) in the gallery

"Tuileries". Three watercolors, all in white frameworks, I bought a long time ago for framing my art.

...After our meeting initiated by mystical tree, Francesco sent me in an envelope of money, $300 - possible participation in the program of AAA: to admit, to compensate... to forget. Or was it my price? There was no text.

Soon after came the letter from Valentina: "Our Gabor... under-married." She has written just such, "under-married". Whom he "under-married", she did not write, but that does not matter. The prefix "under-" brought him closer the edge, which has to cross a matter of time, and while he is not alone, it is a fact.

$300 from Francesco – I spent immediately. On canvas, paper, brushes, and on these, white frames.

"Well, maybe it's for the best. Why such an appendix of memory..."

Scarf... No, probably not need a scarf, shawl enough, yonder. How old is it? ...1988, summer: I go back from Metropolitan (Museum of visual arts); walk along the Fifth Avenue... Right on the ground under a tree a young man sitting, near him are souvenirs, Matrioshky, shawls.

It turns out that the guy with souvenirs - from Russia. I bought from him this shawl for $15.

And I will take a kerchief - to tie my head.

"...Yet it was right on my part: to find Francesco, and ask for forgiveness... for the fact that at one time I sat not in my sled.*(*Russian proverb: "Stay in your own sled!") Not in my class. But now it's not so important..." - I think, putting into the bag my art works for the exhibition.

Yes, now it is not so important. True.

I more often go back by thoughts and by heart to the time of my college youth, and my first love, **S**. It is a pity, what a pity that we then split up, that we were scattered, and it is hardly possible to return.

But going to Paris with my works, I thought, and I knew that after the exhibition in the gallery "Tuileries" I will go to Bulgaria - this is where he, **S**., then returned at the end of the Institute, where he still may live and work. ...In some research institutes... laboratory... Or is he already retired - people grow old so quickly... especially after seventy. He is in his seventies. I will find him, I will see him, will meet him.

But, maybe he is sick? Died? Then I'll sit on the grave, I'll just breath the same air with him.

In Bulgaria! Yes, in Bulgaria. I already became a member of this very, Bulgarian WWOOF. * (* The organization of organic farms, welcoming seasonal workers, volunteers) Will work as a volunteer on an organic farm near Sofia (really do not know the address), then - in Sofia, where he had gone many, many years ago...

August End of August

...In Parisian Metro the ventilation is like hurricane. When someone approached me and offered to help to carry my luggage, I trying to get rid from my hair from the face, shook my head, and this was understood as "no, no, I myself", and I was left alone to drag my burden. Finally, I guessed to tie my head by kerchief, and already on the approaches to the door "Saint Paul" has received assistance in the face of a young man who pulled out my suitcase and my bag with watercolors upstairs. He wished me a good day...

Settled in the hostel* (* hotel-type dormitory where several lodge in a room of people hitherto unfamiliar, often mixed sexes) - thanks to the emergence of "Hostel" and thanks to the Internet, found a hostel online in the Marais. Four bed room, or rather, two bunk-beds room, my bed near the window on the bottom shelf. The room is mixed: my neighbor from the top shelf - girl Inga from Riga, and near the door on the bed sleeping two male individuals.

I put the suitcase under the bed, and - forward, to the gallery.

Found gallery. It turned out, also in Marais, not far; I handed over my art works for the exhibition.

At next morning Inga and I went downstairs for "complimentary" breakfast: toasts, cheese, coffee, etc. When we returned to the hostel room, the two men sleeping now disappeared, to be replaced by two Chinese, one of them Inga clearly liked, she once saw him, a fragile four-eyed (bespectacled) guy, even tone of her voice changed. Vibrato:

- Hia-ah-ah…

Chinese guys left to take shower. Inga sat down with a book at only chair nearly window, to read (I think so), and I - on the bed, to write a letter to my ex-roommate by New York dorm, Olesya, a young girl, who came to New York for some "Students Exchange" then turned out we're not only roommates, but also soul mates, we went together to culture and non-culture objects of New York; because of the resemblance people took us as relatives (mother-and-daughter, sisters, etc.). But to write, and in general it was uncomfortable to sit, if was necessary to straighten - my head was hit about Inga's shelf. I put the letter aside and went out.

I call Lucille - we met on the exhibition in Cannes. Later we long time actively wrote and called by phone to each other. Lucile is so strange: she worried, why she received only silver medal while I received golden? She even asked if it possible to send that golden medal to her Paris address, and she wrote a letter with that request to Director of Salon, Madame Solbes. But the medal was already sent to me in New York. And now Lucile surprised: "Why are you in hostel? I feel offended." We met. Lucille phoned to her acquaintance Solange, who lived in a big apartment, and I might rent a room from her, but Solange was not in Paris, she had such job, said Lucile, something like "commivoyageur", and then Lucille brought me to some director of some atelier, Mimi.

Atelier "RA" is a spacy three-floored house, with a backyard and a garden, outbuilding where I get a room for 300 Euro per month, it's great. Mimi - lady with violet eyes, dark blond unwashed straight hair to the shoulders, and else: talks too much, like stream of speech - in French for Lucille, in English for me. I could hardly able to go into my room to put my belongings.

Still August

"Dear Olesya!

Now I am closer to you, to your Minsk: in Paris! I will participate in exhibition with my three art works. I have three watercolors: "Little Mermaid", "Black Rooster with Little Bell", and "She Walks In Beauty".

Opening will be in three days, and while I walk around the city, and of course, I visit my favorite Luxembourg Gardens. I stayed in the studio of "R. A." I have a cozy room in the lodge. Across from me - a little room rented by Guillaume, a young movie director from Normandy, very good, kind boy. He uses to tell: "All people are beautiful." It is his credo. Can you imagine? The hostess has very interesting friends.

I brought here with me earrings for you, I could not send from New York, but hope to send them from here won't be a problem.

How is your hand?

How is Mitya?

Write me please.

Hugs,

Good bye-.

N."

Olesya injured her hand while working "exchange" in the kitchen Brighton Beach Russian cafe, almost chop off by a bread slicer her thumb (and even of the right hand), and left New York with arm in a sling.

Mitya - a young man, student at the seminary, prepares for monastic life; Olesya in love with him.

On the opening day I got up early – to wash my hair, to put myself in order. Mimi was awake and sat at the entrance to the shower, to the right of the front door. Oh-oh, I feel, I know now she is going to talk, talk, talk, chatter, bursting endlessly about politics, celebrity, about the events of the past days and years... Well, for sure, talks: «What do you think about...» I listened, nodded: "Yes, yes..." Sideway, sideway... slipped in the shower. ...From the shower: "Yes, yes, yes..." Go back heel into my room, nodding by my wet head.

Came to the opening: Lucille and her boyfriend; Mimi and her friends, including an artist - her neighbor at home; photographer from Serbia; the big-nosed French Joan, and Magda... gray-haired Romanian Madalina (so Romanian "Magdalena", but without the "g"). We went back to studio (atelier) together, long distance. Such pleasant company! Only here Mimi! - Should someone on the street to ask about anything, such as "how to get to..." - as began this stream of verbosity. But finally we came. Sat at a table in the hallway... I noticed, the French are not "larks"* (*those who used to get up early), and in general, they spend hours a day at a random. They do not watch at it, I mean, the time...

Tomorrow I will go to the bus station to find out bus schedules to Sofia.

∾

...I went. I knew the schedule. I think to go right at the end of the show. But now - watercolor, paper, and go to my favorite Luxembourg Gardens...

August

Mimi has guests, the same: gray-haired Magda... that is Madalina; photographer from Serbia; Joan the Proboscis; artist-neighbor, and a new face, "Handyman», a stocky man of about sixty, loud-voiced, looks like Sobakevich of Gogol's "Dead Souls" that is "tailored wrong, but tightly sewn". Mimi at the table, as usual, is interested in conversing, and I have to care about making tea and serving guests. Handyman name is Victor (with the accent on "o", as Hugo!). In the gab he does not concede Mimi, quite the contrary. It turns out he is jabberer better than Mimi. In his monologue in French I catch: he is proud to be working, and thus put on the feet of his children - gave them an education. (There are people who for some reason believe that they only ones who have children.) Subject of Mimi - foreign policy, Palestine and the Jews. Artist-neighbor keeps silent, the Serb photographer asked me in a whisper if he could find recognition in the United States.

Gray Madalina draped in silver-gray, in her ears - colorful earrings, her hair pulled back in a bun. I noticed she does not have the upper eyelids. I wonder how she sleeps, with her eyes open, or what? She looks at Victor without blinking with emotion, wanting to get a word in French; now she spoke her word (squeaky voice - some cartoon) – but Victor interrupted... staring at me. Asked - Mimi translated into English - how much are (cost) my works, those that are on display.

-1 000, thousand Euro, but negotiable, I mean I may reduce to five hundred.

I add: I have with me more art works, watercolors with views of Central Park in New York. He thought for a bit:

- Alors... Combien coûtent-ils?* (*So... How much they are?)

- Well, because they are small and without frames -100 and 150 Euro... And I also make watercolors in Luxemburg Gardens. Those are larger. And, of course, are more expensive.

- Alors...* (*So...)

(Thinks to buy?)

When I went to the kitchen for tea, he managed to get out of the table, meet in a narrow passage and tickle me behind the ear, and then to pinch my thigh: "Belle!"*(* Beauty -Fr.) Alors...

Finally, everybody left besides Madalina, she stays - she would spend the night somewhere, somewhere in the second or third floor of the main building, there must be a lot of places. I'm heading toward the lodge... Suddenly Madalina and Mimi are beginning to say after me, to pop duo, Madalina in French, Mimi simultaneously in English; spontaneously this duo invites me to marry Victor, who, as they say, has two or three houses in some Aveyron. Evil smiles...

Well. This is too much... Why would they? Jealous? Politely, as possible polite –do not anger them - I suggest they take for themselves as husband that... with two (three?) houses.

- By the way, is not he married? He says something about his children...

Mimi:

- Divorsed, twice.

- That's good – I smile. – Good night.

Gone, at last, in my room, collapsed on the bed... Phew! Finally! Fall asleep. And somewhere... where great times of youth...

"I am back in Jardin Luxembourg* ..." (*Luxemburg Garden)

"I am back in Jardin Luxembourg …"

I want to write a poem, yet keep this phrase, this first line in my mind, the poem does not come, feel I am not poet, cannot go after this phrase! Dusk is coming. Today – watercolor number… eight… nine?

In South-West corner, by the wall-fence, there bluebells blooming: there is a hill covered by violet bluebells. I have already watercolor "Black Rooster with Little Bell", right now it's hanged in "Tuilerie", there many-many bluebells. I remember them from Moscow forest. And now, in Luxemburg Gardens, I feel like I go back in that Moscow forest. I love. I love this place. O, an idea: "Paris – City of Love…" After finishing my etude I will try to continue my poem on the paper. What, if this way:

"…I love Jardin Luxemburg
And Paris – this city of love…"

Beautiful France! Here, French people are passing. They, French, somehow… like toys. "Bella…"

"I love Jardin Luxemburg…"

- Fermer!* (*we close-Fr.)

That was said, actually, barked, by a young police woman. They close. It's time to. Another word, I have to leave. I am leaving, leaving, no need to look at me that way, stroking a greasy side, where must a gun located.

"I hate all ladies in uniforms –

Nuns, police women, nurse..."

O my, what I am about? It's her, gendarme-in-skirt, inspired me, or, rather gave me idea of such inhuman lines with her "Fermer"... And for some unknown reasons I offended the nurses...

"...and Paris –that city of love..."

No, I am not poet, certainly. Maybe I am a prosaist... But not poet.

- Je pars*. (*I am leaving-Fr.)

~

September

Lucille – a plump, dark eyed cutie, with a new short haircut, rejuvenated her for decades. Entrance hall, bedroom, kitchen - all in canvases a la Jackson Pollock: spray, spray... And - spray. Spray sometimes crossed by a straight line or a triangle. Why she chose this style? I look at these works through the eyes of Khrushchev. In her educational works in gouache and pastels: still life quite decent - good French taste; and there are portraits, good, a lot. But in a prominent place – abstractions.

...Father was an abstract painter, unrecognized, not appreciated by the public, nor his wife - the mother of Lucille. He left, went to the far small town and continued to work. He met a woman who understood him... Few, two or three of his works on the wall at Lucille's - angular design, read as an abstract story about the life of an artist... Why chose his daughter's handwriting, "spray"? But... how she came to the temple of art?

- How you, Lucille, came to the... I mean, how you started to paint?

Lucille history: she was 26 years old and worked as a secretary in the office, lived with her mother and stepfather, and that's... She found and visited her father... Suddenly realized that it is not for her, sitting in the office "from" and "to"; that her interest is brushes and easel... She quit her job... bought a ticket to San Francisco. To find herself!

(I thought of my own impulse to create: it was in Moscow. My classmate - I do not remember the name - invited to see the exhibition of African masks, African art. I went. What I saw was so unusual, so piercing... Since that time, since the day after this show, so to speak, I do not let go off brushes.) In San Francisco, Lucille rented beds, worked as a waitress, on Sundays went to an art studio. She married the old poet. The wedding dress was lilac color. And Cala lilies, her favorite flower. Green Card... Then her father died. She returned to France, in Paris, divorced; rented this studio. Met new friend; found work - again, in the office, part-time, in her free time she's painting, painting, painting...

But why spray?

(Ask Lucille.)

~

Victor again with Mimi. The fact that space of atelier, that is, water, and other terms of communal facilities in poor condition, Mimi whenever invited Victor to help, correct - there is no choice, the neighbor, the artist, whose name is "Zhyan", does not understand anything in this; Serbian photographer - a rare visitor; and there is Victor, who appears late, eats, drinks (by the way, for present time at my expense, I buy wine and French snacks in the store through the block, because Mimi such impractical), says, says, broadcasts a voice of thunder, and returns "home", i.e. to somewhere in his Aveyron or for the night to someone from the Parisians, promising to do everything in the following times.

... O, today he is not alone. Today he is in the company of "Michelle" - grim and untidy lady, more like a vagabond. A couple of times, going for tea in the kitchen, I caught Victor kissing with this Michelle. Maybe she has money, how Mimi could say... I pretend not to notice these symptoms of their mutual affection. Especially that Michelle seems harmless - on the table she is silent, does not support the socialite talk, just nothing. I do not even know her voice.

Ate, drank, gone. Well, I was right: Mimi says Michelle rich widow.

Still September

...Ate-drank-gone. I ask Mimi, what should repair that unblessed Victor, why she was waiting for him - it appears to hang curtain (fallen) on the window to rid dreams Mimi from light street lamps and so on. I insist, and insisted to hang curtain ourselves and for Victor leave others, non-urgent orders. I am going up the steep stairs. Second floor... Third... What a mess, what chaos! Among the rubbish, rags, scraps on the floor, the bed of Mimi. In the corner - half littered with food waste, drawings by R.A. Even in such interior, and in the dim light, these works, black-and white cityscapes - fascinating. Overcoming Mimi's persistent attempts to chat, I succeeded to hang the curtain. Needs Mimi in Victor, I know, will not be affected.

~

Gray Madalina calls me "Ni-noch-ka" making stress on "o"... Now she came to the studio accompanied by athletic African, he said there not far from here will be a concert of a young pianist, invited me to join them, and three of us departed to a house of culture... We go on foot, it's close. African's name is Claude Stone. He is fluent in English, as, indeed, in French also. Here he is behind because of the "little need". Madalina says to me with the help of gestures (afraid I do not understand her French and in English she is "boom-boom*" (*zero), yes, I am not strong in French, but in everyday life Okay, we understand each other), she says that she is in love with this Claude Stone. And colorful earrings in her ears, as well as colorful bracelet on her arm were given by another African, who was with her before Claude Stone. I look at the earrings, bracelet on - it seems to be made of electrical tape. But, apparently, they are dear to her because given her by loved one. He left. To Africa. To his wife and children. Now she's in love with Claude. Claude catches up with us – has urinated somewhere, and we approach to the entrance... Madalina persuades security man to let her go for free as a journalist. (Curious, in which the magazine she works?) She persuaded. But Claude and I pay «donations». The pianist plays brilliantly. Before leaving, we sacrifice another "donation".

"Hello, dear Olesya!

...The opening of the exhibition took place. It was fun, a lot of us, the artists, and many styles were represented. In basement were displayed sculptures of a young Frenchman - oh, it must be seen: the ugly body half-human, half-reptiles... Some tongues, ears... But there were also pleasant works. I liked so much landscapes by one woman, also French, she was at the opening with her adult son. It was touching to see his respect and love for his mother's art. My new friends came at the opening.

I have to admit that I gave the earrings to Madalina, very nice woman from Romania. She calls me "Ninochka", making stress on "o", and she says she knows that in Russian language suffix "chka" - caressing, and yes, she saw a movie about the Russian spy, looking like me, and my namesake, who has the suffix "chka" in her name*... (*"Ninochka") Recently Madalina complained that she lost one earring - memorable (gift from her boyfriend), well, and I felt so sorry for her... I'll buy for you the others..."

∼

September

Jardin Luxemburg...

Atelier "R.A."

All the same, and Victor

Mimi - once again - asks Victor about some Rosalind, his neighbor in the Aveyron. She says that in the past they were friends with Rosalind, and even divided, that

is, shared apartment, then Rosalind something said
or did, and now they are not compatible. Well, if not
friends, why every time to ask about Rosalind. Who of
them said that "something wrong?"

While drinking rose wine - bought by me again -
Victor asked if I could take him with me to New
York: he found airline that can sell two tickets, one of
those - for him of course - free, well, like in the New
York shoe stores on sale: buy one pair of shoes - you
can get another item for half price or even free. Mimi
translated into English, while somehow smiling sweetly.
Smiled all the feasters, big-nosed Joan in her wide smile
even dropped the cigarette from her mouth. I said:

- No, it's too much responsibility, in New York I do not
  have a living space, there I myself rent a bed in the
  dormitory, female dormitory...

("What he's to do there?")

I remembered my roommates by dorm – alive and
deceased, those who still removing a shit in the
chamber pots and swabs from the flabby crazed old
men and women, and those that turned to ash in
Coney Island * (* Southern District of New York) the
crematorium for the poor... Nadya... No, first Vera.
Vera - a neighbor across the bed on the right, passed
away after Nadya, and Coney Island hospital, rather
Crematorium of hospital could not find the address of
her son – to report ...

Nadya – my neighbor by bed from left – came to New York from Moscow through some Moscow Agency, in hopes to make money and help her son. When she arrived to New York, the employers who met her took away her passport. She began to work with sick old man.

Once she met a young construction worker, also illegal like her, little older than her son and much younger than she was. She fell in love deeply, she dedicated to him her simple-minded poetry – full journal; she gave him expensive gifts... The old man died – she moved to old sick lady, took care of her... Another old lady... Then she got sick herself, finally visited doctor to examination: cancer, already non-operable. Young lover left her, she wrote about this few bitter poems. She spent three more years without job, money, documents, paying for dorm bed by rare cleaning works and eating what people give her or what she manages to steal from dorm's refrigerator: bread, milk, coffee... Once she received a letter about sudden death of her son in Moscow, collapsed... died. Oh, actually this idle company should not know all this. They understood only my first word, "NO". The rest would be for them not understandable and not interesting.

Feast continued. That strange idea with ticket for Victor to New York seemed kind of foolish joke. In cases like this, I feel I am given to understand that I am a stranger.

How good could be sell even one watercolor... I need so much to go to Bulgaria.

The room has a lot of old magazines, different. In one of them I came across the picture: snakes, a lot. Under the picture: «Personnel féminin amical». Translated: "The friendly female staff" I remembered duet Mimi and Madalina about Victor with his Aveyron houses... Then their jokes, exchanging meaningful glances at the table, smiling. Oh-oo-oo-oh... But... Nevertheless, Madalina, in my opinion, is very nice person. However, I do not understand why she had taken from me earrings with sour face. In my opinion, it is a decent gift. I bought them in New York City, in Greek jewelry shop thinking about Olesya, Olesya just on the eve of her departure from New York lost one earring, and that's... two transparent stones, as two tears. But Madalina slipped the earrings silently into her purse, and not wearing.

Madalina is from Romania, 53, a journalist - so she introduced herself. On business cards, which she distributes (I have already 5, gives again and again, just a reflex of some sort) it is written: «Journaliste». Arrived in Paris, where she rents a room or a studio; for a living she does some "Romanian massage". Now her cell phone ringing, she appoints a massage, writes down the address, negotiating some other details in French. Artist

"Zhyan" shakes her knee, winks, gesture of approval: thumb up.

~

September.

I am at Lucille. Drink wine – red, local, cheap, because local. Delicious!

The story of first love: Lucile was 16, and she came to the summer vacation for a week in Nice to her aunt - the sister of her mother. On the last day strolling on the promenade met him... Rustle of waves: "Je t'aim..." "Je t'aim..." * (* I love you, Fr.) Moonlight... Thorny sand... She returned to Paris as woman. He did not call. She missed him. A month later, under some pretext she went to Nice again... came to the embankment and saw him in the company of his wife and two children: friendly four. He led the procession. He did not notice her or did not recognize.

She wept, remembering. We were silent...

("But my first love - my last love. As soon as the show is over...")

After another "health" and "chin-chin" (or "rank-rank") Lucille says:

- I have an idea, that is, the dream: to gather artists among the six, well, five... and buy a house, team house. Country house! Some of these five will live permanently, some from time to time. House!!

- Great idea! I am for! Let's look at houses for sale in Bulgaria!

- In Bulgaria! Why Bulgaria? It is so far from Paris.

- What do you want - a cheap house near Paris! Do not make me laugh! Let's take a look online!

- Well... I still do not understand why in Bulgaria. Yes... Oh, no.

Sep, 2009

Poème d'amour

...Claude Stone, Stone Claude Claude Stone, Stone Claude.....

Elle vient de jouer avec les mots qui composent son nom prénom,

prénom nom, nom-prénom!

Il est beau Claude Stone, Stone Claude, Claude Stone...

(A love poem

... Claude Stone, Stone Claude Claude Stone, Stone Claude.....

It's just a play on words that made up from his first name and his last name,

First name, last name, first name!

It's beautiful: Claude Stone, Stone Claude, Claude Stone *...)

(* Engl. Claude - cloud, Stone - stone)

... And all in the same spirit. "Poem" is written by Madalina. Next - the same as at the beginning: "Claude Stone Stone Claude Claude Stone..." etc.

We made friends with her enough to trust each other personally. I let slip the reason for my craving for Bulgaria... Then she asked me what I think about Victor. Why is not about Claude Stone.

"About Victor? ...Nothing."

"Nothing?"

"Well... He..."

"He has blue eyes?"

"Uh-huh, blue, really"

(And really, blue, dark blue almost, almost like **S.**
Perhaps it's... like reincarnation, in such wrong tailored,
but tightly knit body - blue eyes, almost blue. Oh,
but...)

What is waiting for me in Bulgaria? Lucille did not
want to hear about Bulgaria because, in her words, "it is
so far from Paris." Madalina is in love with this athlete,
Claude Stone. And, it turns out, with Victor as well.
(And Mimi – with Victor too...)

Claude Stone not responding to Madalina's calls and
any invitation. He did not want then, after the concert,
come to her for a cup of coffee, referring to the fact that
he has to get up early morning tomorrow. He is "gay,"
says Madalina. She will go to Romania with Victor, so
as soon as Victor freed (from what?). And he'll drive her
to Romania for a week.

∽

In the room of atelier/studio "R. A.", I dreamed about
Inna: *I'm in the Luxembourg Gardens. I see Inna.
She goes to the exit-gate briskly, clutching a stack of my
watercolors. I shout "Inna!" She does not respond, go
faster. I think after her: "So, she was pretending that she
could not walk fast..." I want to catch up. I do not have
time to catch up* - woke up. Remember: Inna long dead.

Cannot wait when the exhibition be over

September

Today in the atelier only ladies, three of them: Mimi, Madalina (M&M), and big-nosed Joan.

The big-nosed Joan over fifty, French, was married with famous photographer (I already saw his art works, black-white) much older than herself, they divorced a long time ago. And recently, he was brought in the hospital in a state of scientifically "Alzheimer", in Russian it's also called often "marasmus". Now she goes to visit him in hospital. - Mimi says, because of the inheritance, but she says such in the absence of Joan, and with her Mimi says that now she, Joan, have occupation: nurse; so now – Mimi says – Joan will not remain without work.

Joanne smokes a lot, just does not let the cigarette from her mouth (except for a smile, but it happened only once so far). And this is probably all you can say about her.

Generally in this company and around, basically there women; only few males: neighbor artist "Zhyan" is seen here less and less, photographer Serb has disappeared, probably, found recognition in a different place, and one man - the axis of rotation: Victor. (He a couple of times tickled me behind the ear, probably in gratitude for dinner... And pinched my thigh. Such is Aveyronian supply of male attention.)

Guillaume do not count: he avoids this company.

Mimi and Madalina, that is, M & M, told that Victor volunteered to take me sometime in Aveyron, in Aveyron are galleries, a lot. Joan nodded, chewing, however, her cigarette. Marriage and other things they did not offer. I smiled in response, thanked... I promised to think: Well, yes, we should not forget about secularism.

~

I'm back in the Luxembourg Gardens.

At the height of bird flight - a giant bowl of petunias. All shades of purple petunias hanging down, looking on the bottom of the stretched space. Rather, on the ditch: the greens, pond... And outside the Garden, away - block of new buildings and bright green domes of trees. I draw. I remember different things.

I remember my mother: petunias were her favorite pot flowers, and while she was alive, all shades of purple petunias adorn windowsills in our hut.

Mimi told yesterday about herself: seventies, Englishwoman transformed into a Frenchwoman, a former waitress, as young girl went to the States, where he worked in New York McDonald's; married a man much older than she. (Why all they marry men much older than themselves?) Became pregnant - has decided to get rid of the fetus, something went "wrong", removed the uterus, remained fruitless. Arriving in Paris, she met a man, that is, another man, and they began to live together. They lived together badly. She met with R.A. - came to him in the studio and complained to life and boyfriend. R.A. let her stay in the atelier - a lot of places... Then he became ill, his sculptures - snapshots from different parts of his own body, including the head, face: as a result of mold damaged his lungs. Mimi visited him in the hospital, and when he died, stayed in the studio, and no force may knock her out (it's not her words but mine) — neither so-called authorities (French authorities) nor the ex-wife of the sculptor, nor even his nephew Nicholas who is also a sculptor. For all her incompetence in the arts and in business Mimi finds some ways to diminish the rights of the former wife of R.A. and humiliate Nicholas depicting him an idiot, unable to control the company. Nicholas lives in Brittany. A couple of years ago, Mimi allowed him to bring his work and arranged the exhibition. Nicholas' art works on the shelves, in the aisle; his theme - birds, media - ceramics. Mimi laughs, pointing at the sculpture: "Look! Coop!" She runs to a lawyer, for advises how to defend "the art gallery and museum" - as she calls the studio late. And she is obviously in love with Victor.

∿

September morning

... I went to the Bois de Boulogne. It turned out not so wild a place as it seemed, perhaps because it was the day. At the entrance to the "forest" was a pavilion that was celebrated some French Day, and they have a lot of French Days. After the speeches (I have not understood), came the hour of white wine, I also got a plastic glass of wine. I was holding my plastic glass of wine and mumbling in response to attempts by local gentlemen to discuss the events of the Day. Then I wandered behind the pavilion and sketched a wildly-blooming pink bush of unfamiliar to me plant.

∾

Francine

... Call to Atelier Francine, whom I met a year ago in a plane on my return from Cannes. She flew to New York on the ticket purchased online, and I showed her the memorial places. Recently I sent her email - found a library near the studio, and there computers. Now, Francine goes out of her small town, somewhere not very far from Paris to see me and her son, who is working in police in Paris. Great news! I invited Francine in the studio. Mimi was off somewhere, most likely in a cafe across the street, where the Arabs give her free meal for her fiery speeches in favor of Palestine.

Francine came and asked me to cook something like
hot soup, scrambled eggs... I had to disappoint her:
"...the studio in the status of the museum, the studio
had no utensils for cooking, all you may only have -
a cookie, salad, tea from the kettle". We drank by a
cup and went to the gallery. There skinny, flirtatious
Francine, in her short skirt and painted eyes creepy
looking like an old cat, flirted with gallery owner,
giggled in front of my paintings as if it were a comic
book, not product of fine art. We looked at show and
gone. On the way back we had a drink in a café by
glass of cider... I walked her to the subway "Glasier",
where her son was waiting her in his police car, and I
went to the Luxembourg Gardens. There are interesting
sculptures, historical, symbolic. That is "Liberation":
from what? The sculptural composition: two male
figures, one man support another, falling man. I paint
"Liberation" in watercolor. Now, watercolor pictures of
Luxembourg Gardens I have plenty... On the way back
I stopped to the Arabs near Metro "Bayonnet", here,
not far from monument Edith Piaf and her café, i.e. of
her debuts, - telephone and computer facilities. These
young Arabs, all services on their place not expensive...
I'm calling by phone to the organic farm.

... Finally, the woman picked up the phone, the voice is
not too dear.

"This is Maria?"

"N-no." (Hard to hear.)

"Who?"

"... Uh... Vera."

I tell her:

"Could you tell me your address? I may come to Sofia by bus, but the bus, all buses come to Sofia at 2 am..."

She:

"Come, we meet."

Address is not told.

Hung up.

After that telephone communication I went by foot to Per Lachaise, this time - for the umpteenth time! - hoping to find the grave of Edith Piaf. It was still rather deserted, so coming inside I began fearing ...

There are a lot of ravens: although they do not get human flesh (I think), they feel the true owners of the cemetery. Maybe saturated with the spirit of the dead? Here, one such flew from the roof of some noble tomb of some past century Frenchman; flew pass me on the level of my head; moved to a tree branch of the mighty old poplar. ...Oh! Roses! Fresh roses on the hill! I approach; read: grieving relatives - grave strewn with roses for Marie Trintignant - actress, untimely deceased, or rather killed, by her drunken lover.

Edith Piaf grave, I never found.

Still September.

Lucille invited to look at the outskirts of Paris show-festival of flowers, namely dahlias. I remembered school days: September 1; children come to school with bouquets of autumn flowers, among them - the magnificent dahlias...

After looking dahlias, we sat down on the shore of lake, looking at the ducks swimming on the lake. Lucille:

- How's Mimi?

- Oh, that Mimi. Never mind. She is talking too much. Just awful! And more... Imagine, I come recently – see a note from her, inviting me to an Arab cafe across the street, where her "old friends"... I went into that café: Mimi has supper in the company of two young men, one was described as "an old friend" collector named Andre, a second - young Gallery owner. Gallery owner's name is Vincent. Vincent - Jew and Mimi somehow talked quite obscene things about Jews, meanwhile devouring the dish for which he paid. Vincent expressed a desire to take a look at my portfolio. He and I went to the studio, I mean Atelier; I pulled out my portfolio. He said that he likes, but it can be so accepted among gallery owners to say. I asked him why he suffers abuse by Mimi, which now dines for his expense. He said he is concerned about the business and the gallery business goes bad... Mimi called him - wants to sell something from sculptural works, and he came and introduced to her Andre. Then he asked whether the color of my hair is natural, I said "yes", he asked for permission to touch my hair... He touched my hair. Then he asked, what is my weight? I hesitated a little bit, not knowing what to say, and in general, in kilograms or pounds, but then, fortunately (for me), Mimi flew in. She apparently was afraid that I have something of selling my work without her and she ran, munching on the go her "course", her dish. However, anti-Semitic outpourings continued... I went to my room and do not know what it was all over.

- Yes, but... Before you one friend of mine, artist from Germany Petra, stayed with her. And she was terrified of Mimi. She, Petra, had to feed someone together with Mimi... What else...

- A, it may be, Victor... Handyman. He's there at Mimi emeritus eater.

- Looks like him.

... In the wing, in the room opposite of mine - young video director Guillaume, whose motto is: "All the people are beautiful.") His videos - also on this subject. Here is one of them, he shows once again: one American girl, nice-looking brunette, has decided to improve her appearance: she dyed blonde, lost N number of pounds, and passed through a series of plastic surgeries that result looked like a skinny plastic doll from the store "99 cents" for the poor. Here she took the stage in such indecent form, crying with joy, her relatives hugging her and crying, too, for some reason, with widely gaping mouths and showing molars... Guillaume said that his girlfriend also wanted to make a "plastic" – to shorten her nose, but he told her that he will stop all relations with her if she would do this "plastic". And he, Guillaume, divinely beautiful: dark straight hair to his shoulders; straight nose, brown almond eyes... He likes my portfolio. He wants to go to the gallery to look at the work of "alive". When friends of Mimi come, he disappears, as he says, "to breathe." Funny, wise, kind boy...

∾

Lucille phoned (Mimi is not very kindly handed me the phone – I need to get own phone, a mobile phone), and invited to exhibition dedicated to winemaking. This exhibition is only one day show - rural, Lucille participates there. "With her spray," - so I thought. And I was not mistaken.

We went there with Guillaume. We rode an hour and a half by train. Arrived... And then, in the premises of the local mayor's office, in a narrow long corridor – we

see pictures, pictures, collages... I must say, the style of
Lucille suited to the topic of the show: her paintings,
two of them - flashes of red, alluring, fragrant wine,
marvel, miracle.

Another miracle: from the hallway - access to a very
broad area with stairs leading down to the building
and to the courtyard of the local school. From platform
overlooking: the school yard, surrounded by pink
flowers. The gates of yard were wide open, and from
the area illuminated by the early sunset, it seemed: here
it is - the entrance to paradise. O, blessed flowers of
France! Lucille says, they unpretentious, all semi-wild.

Bulgarian in Paris

Lucille said, near Saint Michel is a boat on the Seine,
and in it, in the boat, painting exhibition of Bulgarian
artist. Tomorrow there is an opening. Lucille will not
be able to go - she needs to take works from wine show.
Guillaume also has some business. Would I go? What a
question! Of course, this is *Bulgarian* show!

... And I went. Interesting work, pleasant color
abstraction, and most importantly, I do not remember
anything, except that nice color. Specifically to recall
the color turned out too impossible. The artist herself -
blooming beauty and outgoing young lady in some folk
costume: long skirt embroidered blouse; vest. (Lucille
said, this exhibition, as well as other, sponsored by a
rich lover of Bulgarian beauty.) In the corner sat two,

one of them told pleasant things in English with a slight accent. It turned out that they are the Bulgarian writer Marco R. and German photographer (his name, seems, Rainer)... I joined their conversation. (Everybody switched to Russian.) I said that I am waiting for the end of the exhibition in the "Tuileries", then by bus to go to Bulgaria, to volunteer at the farm... Soon.

- Which farm?

- Organic. Only now, though, strangely, when I called, a woman picked up the phone, and she said her name "Vera", while online she was "Mary." And then, the bus according to the schedule arrives in Sofia at 2 am, she said, will meet it at 2am. But the farm address she does not say...

Marco takes from me the phone number of "Vera— Mary". and gives it to sitting near girl "Iliana", his secretary:

- Come on, find out...

Iliana went out... Returned... Marco:

- I think that we saved your life.

("Wow. I did not think that organic farms are a threat to life. What am I going to do?")

Came out from the boat, three: Marco, Iliana, I. (German left early.) Group of Japanese-geisha girls with bright make-up caught up with us and shoved - for some reason to me - a flyer * (* leaflet) - invitation for their party. Marco and I laughed: why me and not to the young generation represented by Iliana? Do I look like one of the... Japanese girl, geisha?

Parting - we had been seen in front of us over the Seine, Notre Dame de Paris, a favorite place and the spectacle of Marco. Marco gave me his book about Paris. Book - pictures and stories. Pictures - memorial sites; a meeting with the French celebrities - Sylvie Vartan, Nicolas Sarkozy, etc; text laced with admiration and love to Paris.

Bulgarian in Paris... In Paris... Bulgarian...

... That night I dreamed of Bulgaria as a huge blossoming neglected garden. I sketched that dream garden.

September...

Yesterday Madalina invited me to listen to a lecture at the Sorbonne. We came, took our places. Madalina started calling by phone to Claude Stone, he probably did not answer, and she left him a message - invitation to a lecture. After boring speeches, time came for lecturer' "questions and answers". Madalina in her low-cut dress asked questions, leaning forward and deliberately pulling down shoulders straps; it was funny: a serious face - and shoulders, chest, breast exhibited... Between the questions and answers in a whisper she told me that yesterday she overslept with African boy - a teenager from her home. He seems super, or the son of super, or someone else.

- Can you imagine!! He is half the age of my son!

She has a son 30 years old, he, of course, too, not in Romania.

- Well... ("30: 2 = 15 . 15? Crazy, or what?") It is now your new boyfriend?

(Something it was necessary to say in response.)

- O... What are you! I will meet him ("you mean, sleep with him" – I correct her mentally) a couple of times, and all. In general, I cannot date men ("15 - man?") more than four times. Sh-sh-sh... Ecute! * (*Listen)

("It's something... something not quite... Still wondering for which a magazine she works, in the sense, writes...")

~

E-mail came from Olesya

"Good afternoon!

I'm happy for you: you are surrounded by such good people.

And I have good news, even two:

Mitya...talked. He loves me too!

My hand is alright, removed the bandage."

September also

At Lucille

Lucille asked her boyfriend to cook something, he is such excellent cook. And he is also great dancer – they met on the dance floor, and here they are together, there is a "boyfriend and girlfriend," or, as the Americans say they «couple» * (* pair).

We drink delicious local red wine, joking: "Expensive", as much as 3 Euro! Something ends on «... eau». Lucille says - her boyfriend in the kitchen - about love and farewell night with one Newzellander... a few days ago. His image: sketched hastily as farewell... Where they met?

- ... Just met the night before his departure... It was snowing outside... All night.

- What "snowing"? This is serene Indian summer.

- I mean the rain.

- Ah... would you see him again, someday?

- Hardly. Long away... Expensive.

("Kind of Love's meteorite...")

- What a tasty wine.

September noon

The company at the table – Mimi and Madalina - this duet, alliance M & M. Guillaume in the passage leading to the fligel, that is in the same courtyard, garden, sweeping - Mimi accounted to him for duty. Victor arrives, eating-drinking and repeats - in the first person - offer to take me to Aveyron. Visiting French galleries in Aveyron is tempting, except that Victor's company seems scary. He is not relative man. He is stranger, to be honest. I asked Guillaume, can I go in Aveyron, and, most importantly, with the Victor, or not to go. Guillaume, putting aside his broom, gives OK:

- I think, he's just primitive, but no more. Not dangerous.

He gave his phone number just in case. M & M our conversation and persuasion do not hear, and Victor in English does not understand. (Actually, our contact with Guillaume they do not like.) Lunch continues and turns into dinner. I asked Victor how far we go - it's getting dark. He says, go for a long time, but there is his friend Rosalind, I may spend the night at hers, and tomorrow - the galleries. At the mention of the name of Rosalind Mimi hurries to send her regards. ("The friendly female staff" "Personnel féminin amical»)

Aveyron – where is it? Provence? I do not know geography, absolutely, and forgot to ask Guillaume.

... Here, finally set off. At the last moment I laid out my work, leave with me a portfolio - enough to represent.

It's getting dark. Ride...

Describing the experience of night trip - needed to paint, France is beautiful at all times of day and year.

... We stopped in a cafe by the way satisfy the hunger by coffee and pastry cakes. (I paid.) En route again. Victor hummed, even more, roaring: "La-la-la-la-la..." - interrupting music CDs and demonstrating full absence of musical hearing.

He put a couple of times his paw on my knee. Well... to endure. I just moved on my seat closer to the door... a nap on my seat.

...I opened my eyes: Morning. We go. This is Aveyron, reminding Tara from "Gone with the Wind" * (* a novel by Margaret Mitchell), by redness of the soil. Lots of hills and hills, in some places covered with vegetation, and in some places - looks out the ground' redness. Victor says that we are directed to Rosalind, who is now on the "flea-market", that is, something sells. Going, going... Wildness... And came we to some kind of fence, along the fence are people, a lot, and next - on the ground, mixed with dried or trampled plants, sheep and dog droppings, lying on sale items - books, toys, old clothes... This is Rosalind, Victor points: overweight elderly lady, near her on the ground old magazines.

Victor:

- Bon jour.

Rosalind:

- Bon jour.

He unloads a bag with my extra clothes.

- Où sont vos aquarelles? * (* Where are your watercolors?)

- J'ai le dossier, il suffit de... * (* And I have a portfolio that is enough for...)

Loud claps by the door of the car, he is leaving. I stand next to Rosalind, pecking my nose from fatigue.

In the evening we are at Rosalind place. Her apartment is on the second floor of a plank house. It seems that the first floor is not habited, that is, no apartments, but there are some auxiliary (storages etc.). Rosalind speaks good English, with British articulation. She shows my little room, asks to pay.

- How much?

- 10 Euro per night. You would be here for how long?

- I hope for one night. Maybe two... It depends on how soon I'll be brought to the gallery.

- Uh-huh.

I pay for two nights - just in case.

∽

... I am at Rosalind place third day. We went to super market and bought food. No news from Victor. I'll pay for two more nights. Rosalind could not take me anywhere, she is ill: diabetes. The place where her house – it's a farm, bowery, no other way to tell. Victor, she said, too, lives in a small bowery, and Aveyron - is a region that includes towns and villages such as Rodez... In general, she said, it is the West Pyrenees. She allowed me call to Guillaume. But, she says, she, that is, her phone will soon be cut off for non-payment.

I call Guillaume.

- Hi, Guillaume.

- Well, how?

- So far, nothing. I'm still at place of his lady friend.

(About his paw on my knee did not speak. Yet this is not the most terrible gesture.)

Rosalind - also Englishwoman turned into French, like Mimi. Perhaps they are from the same village, and perhaps, even likely they met in New York, where Mimi was a waitress and Rosalind journalist in one of the many New York "media". Rosalind now retired, living out, as she says, in the Aveyron. She has a daughter in New York, the former. "How it is, the former daughter?" - I ask. "The former daughter held a series of operations to change sex and become a man, that is, son, - says Rosalind. - But to call the son who was born as daughter - it's hard... it is difficult to get used to it"

It seems Rosalind is not silly. And not talkative. "Something is not right," put an end to the friendship between her and Mimi, it was most likely said Mimi.

But I do not quite understand what it is, Rosalind, is obliged to Victor. (Ah, 10 Euros per night...)

... Rosalind offers to play cards, meanwhile, remarks that I am very tidy and flexible (ability to get along?). Here on the eve of, Viktor brought to her for a week Michelle, that was a terrible slut and beech. ("Michelle?

A-a, Michelle…") I lose. I go out to breathe. Around -
old one-and-two-story huts. Delicate flowers at the
walls. I come back, ask a piece of paper, drawing a
flower seen near the house, for Rosalind as a keepsake.

The fourth day - I was begging, and finally, I implore
Rosalind show me the way to the railway station... She
called by phone, and she found - someone drove me to
Rodez. I bought a ticket to Paris. Rode at night, sitting
near the window; passengers came in and out, came
in and out... Paris Station. Morning. Atelier "R. A."
Almost home! The first thing I have to do – buy the
phone, mobile, let it be for a little while, but - enough
to depend on others. I'll phone Rosalind, to say that I
am alright.

During my absence here came a young girl from the
United States, Michelle (another Michelle!) -a film
director, she made a short film, and wants to present
to some festival. The film is about a girl in love,
perhaps autobiographical. A loving girl laments to her
beloved that no one buys her shoes, and intentionally
leads him past the shoe shops. He keeps silent, not
knowing or not understanding the hint. The end. The
show took place in a room of Guillaume. For Michelle
is important to know the opinion of Guillaume.
Guillaume - and I agree with him - believes that shoes
cannot be the measure of relations or feelings. After all,
we do not know the financial condition of the hero, her

beau. Michel promised to think. Maybe she will make a sequel.

She showed us the film and left; spent the night somewhere on the second or third floor of the main building on a heap of rags and went to some friends... I walked her to the Metro.

...Lucille calls, to say that she encourages me to show my portfolio in the gallery two blocks from her house, where she saw passing by, figurative works, so I definitely have to appear there. This "recommendation" was said by tone, not tolerating objections. In the end, I took my portfolio and went to Lucille, and then together we went to this gallery. Something told me that the visit was most needed her, Lucille than me... We came. There in the hall hung a semi-abstract works of some Japanese author. Lucille introduced me to Gallery owner - grim masculine lady. She looked at me - not at the portfolio, and cut off:

- Our gallery - not for foreigners.

- But here you have Japanese' exhibition...

- She has a residence permit. And then...

Lucille hurried with their portfolio (where it came from?)

- Mais, regardez, mon travail... * (* But, look, my work...)

I came out not to interfere with the transaction.

E-mail from Rosalind: Victor was very upset that I left so suddenly. Upset?... The next day - a call to my new "mobile": Victor, his thunderous voice. He's in Paris. He wants to show me the famous temple in Montmartre, Cathédrale du Sacré-Coeur (Sacred Heart Cathedral). I do not know why I agreed to come to the meeting place and the show, but what's done is done. And I came. He was waiting, dressed in faded blue-gray shirt with white patterns.... Took my hand and led me up the stairs upstairs to the temple. We passed the artists of Montmartre. I noticed a lot of good and genuine works rather than souvenir pictures on the memory as the central streets of New York. In the church Victor constantly crossed, and it looked pathetic and weird. On leaving the church, he said it was time for lunch, and bought in the shop downstairs a loaf of bread. Biting from the loaf, eating on the run, broke off a piece to me. (Is it lunch?) Eating his loaf, he slapped me a kiss on both my cheeks - so it is accepted by the French. On this our meeting ended. He went to some challenge, something to fix. I went back, thinking: this man is cloumsy * (* awkward, clumsy), but not so bad, he probably wanted to apologize for the way that it happened with Aveyron galleries. Good gesture. Man's attention. Of course, I could abandon that rendezvous* (*date-Fr.). But it seems to have worked my feminine essence.

Last week of September

I wake up.

The end of the exhibition. Need to take down my works. Nothing is sold and, therefore, not is bought.

And my idea with Bulgaria – just a dream.

In Paris - Indian summer continues. I will make a couple of watercolors. Today I came to the park Monceau (Parc Monceau). On a grass, picnics of French crowd. Dressed in colorful clothes, they looked like flowers of Indian summer scattered on the meadow. I photographed, and then went deep into the park to draw flowers.

On arrival in the studio: Mimi says that Victor offers to go back to his Aveyron and that this time - the galleries; he is now at some Parisian flea-market sells toys, not far, she said address. I went to look for. ...To find was not difficult. Indeed, the Flea Market: Victor laid out for sale a lot of toy automobiles; few teenagers came up to him and bought. Beside him stood the very untidy and silent rich widow Michelle - apparently he with his little cars spent the night at her place. We exchanged nods with her in greeting. I told Victor that

I will gather in the road, and paid to him an advance for the trip... then said goodbye to Guillaume. As I have now acquired a mobile phone, we will be in contact with him without any problems. (And to be afraid of Victor was funny.) In the last minute I left in the studio, tucked under the mattress my documents - passport, bank card, etc. - You never know what, right? I took with me only the cash in my wallet. And I took my watercolors - everything, New York and Paris, among them my favorite, Luxembourg Gardens.

❧

"Dear Olesya!

I am writing after the event, which might be called: 'The Aveyron's motives...'"

❧

Departed at nightfall, again. Again, "La-la-la..." But he seems to have noticed my distaste for his singing – and paused. Tired, or maybe not in the spirit - no paws at my knee, no spontaneous kiss. Well, it's good. Tomorrow - walk through the galleries! I should look good... fell asleep.

... We arrived early in the morning, and this time to his bowery, his house. Actually, one of the three, the least collapsed, stone house. In fact, there the ruins of the two, a pile of stones, and one house more or less intact. Below – kitchenette, dining room and a toilet-shower.

Residential floor is the attic. Go up the stairs, then walk along the very edge of the hole and get into the room with one small window and a low ceiling. There Victor showed me a bunch of fresh washed rags on some couch and said:

Repassé!* (* Iron!-Fr.)

I ironed... ironed, ironed... I ironed all rags. He rose again to show how to fold T-shirts and towels. I was folding, thinking: "Poor old bachelor..." Imagined myself for a while the mistress of the house. It would be fun! Only I would have done differently entrance to the second floor, i.e. level, more secure. O! Imagine furious, full of envy M&M... Ha-ha-ha! Brrr...

- Allons-y! (Go!)

That's voice of real man... He took me with my watercolors into his car. Allons-y! Go!

...And we came. But not in the gallery, but, as it turned out, to a woman, an Englishwoman named Ann, living in the same dilapidated large house. How I understood she underpaid him for some furniture (wardrobe, table, etc.) brought by him sometime and from somewhere. Ann offered to pay in installments, but he wanted it all at once. The conversation was in French. Ann's French was not stronger than mine. I suggested Victor to agree to take parts, and I exchanged a few words with Ann in English, and I must say,

Victor could not stand the English language, thus the fact of our short dialogue in English with Ann led him into a rage. He shouted, waving his arms, approaching Ann. I gave them to understand themselves, came out and began to admire the flowers in the road near the car. Picked up blooming pink yarrow... He jumped out Ann's house and ordered:

- Dans la voiture! * (*In the car!)

We ride (and now I'm afraid to talk and ask). But... he turns around - and again to Anne; took part of the money-receipt made... Ride again - arrived at a factory where a lot of wood... Immerses in the car some blocks; then drives to his home; unloads... Grumbling, farting, unloaded, dragging into building. I even tried to help, but he pushed me away, saying "I myself". Unloaded, took into the house my watercolors... Made an omelette from eggs, which I bought on the way from Paris:

- Manger! * (* to eat!)

Choking, I shared with him a meal... Day to a close. I went outside - looked to see if any Gallery nearby - not seen anything like the gallery – just bedraggled farm. And during trips to the countryside there was no sign of galleries, no galleries. Day is close to the end. I say: «Victor, je vais revenir à Paris» («Victor, I want return to Paris"), he replies, that he brought me - he is obliged to take back. ("Well, that's how I visited Aveyron, I old fool. Soon he will go?")

... Now he is busy with some chocks; again fart. ("How is it in Frenchy! And how it occurred to me to believe that...")

... Finally, takes my bag, carries to the car...

- Dans la voiture! Allons-y!*(* In the car! Let's go!)

He closes the door of his house.

Obeying, I get in the car, but... my works? He closed them in his house!

- Mais mes aquarelles... Mais mes aquarelles... Vous avez oublié... ouvrez, mon travail là-bas... Ouvrez, s'il vous plaît... * (* But my watercolors... But my watercolors... you forgot... Open my work... Open up, please...)

He picks up speed - racing not responding... And the car is followed by a swarm of fireflies from somewhere (in September!). Quickly - darkness; in the darkness flashing fireflies, but he silently rushes forward, forward on a crazy speed... Fireflies swarm not inferior in speed. I repeat, in broken French demand to return, open the door, take my work, it was all so unexpected and so incredibly... I grab the phone from the bag:

- Vous êtes voleur! Je m'appeal a police!* (* You thief! I'm calling the police!)

And though I do not know telephone number of "police", my statement acted in such a way that he pulled out of my hand bag, opened the car door and threw me out on the run, I lay sprawled on the road, and he moved over me, over my legs by his car. I heard my own bloodcurdling scream... Here the swarm of fireflies flashed scarlet fireworks!! Temporary fear of our driver, who gave a little back up, let me grab the open door, pull myself up on my hands, with lightning speed to dive into the car and cling to, and held the seat... He, I think, did not expect such vitality and continuing to drive with his left hand (fireflies - swiftly followed by his car), by his right elbow, he pushes, hits me in the shoulder and chest, and face... Then rummaging in my bag; rakes money from my purse... Took everything, emptied my purse. Escort by fireflies, still there, still there.

- Passeport! Où est tes passeport?* (* Passport! Where is your passport?)

("Somewhere I've heard about it... about my passport... in English... A-ah… from Francesco...")

I do not react, just groaning of pain. Again he tries to push me, but I'm holding on, gripped the seat...

... On the road again hits me in the face and chest, mumbles something, at first, I understood, about the difficulties of his life or work: «travail, travail...», and something about his higher education, «education plus

»... Then he, thinking (if the word "thinking" is suitable for a given person), slowed down in some cafes and asks a young Arab to call for me an ambulance, allegedly involved in a road accident, I hear the word "aksidan" (accident), I had an accident and he picked me up... saved....Watching me so that I did not tell the truth. Ambulance arrived, I was taken to the nearest station, and he - going behind on his car, he holds my bag, where keys, portfolio, my IDs. I have no money, and I do not know where I am... I asked the guys: "He's there? "" Yes, he's following us, "- they respond. They speak English. May I tell them? ...If to say? ...But... we arrived. He, again, near me, holding my bag and watching my every word and gesture. ...X-rayed, tied up (had to cut my left leg jeans soaked with blood - fractured ankle, an open wound); written directions and recipes... "Savior" pays small cash, which he took out of my own wallet. I could not catch moment, when he will turn away - all over me, with my bag in hand, I do not know where I am, I know only that back to Paris I will have to return by his "vehicle", maybe now will not kill, shall not, I think.

...On the road again hits me in the face and chest, again mumbles about difficulties of his life or work «travail, travail...», and something about his higher education, «education plus»... Then, shoving me in the side mumbles that I should immediately leave to New York, do not go to the police, otherwise he would say that I've been involved in prostitution, and the police will believe him. And yet, several times repeated some "profite" (?)... In silence, within minutes, I read a prayer to myself... Dawn. The building of "R.A." He opens the door - dumped me on the asphalt; after me - my bag... He is gone.

I climb, jump on the right foot - it got less injured than left, I hold on to the wall of the house, open the door... Crawling towards the wing... Crawling towards the room... Here is the bed. Painfully! My watercolors, my art works...

~

"... In the studio just for a day/night of my absence Guillaume gone - as it turned out, Mimi immediately after I left kicked him out, to find fault with him because of something, and kicked out, but there was a nephew of R. A. Nicholas, a sculptor. He took part in me: called a taxi to the hospital; took a pair of crutches, without crutches I couldn't later move ever. He brought me coffee and something to eat. Mimi - I did not write that she hosted in the studio and did not want her place was taken by Nikolay? - She said that everything that happened is "a misunderstanding" and other nonsense..."

~

Late Morning... Doorbell rings, voices in the hallway... I clench with fear, Victor suddenly or someone like him

· came to me to finish. A knock at the door: in the room comes a slim middle-aged man with a beard "goatee", smiles:

- Something wrong? Something hurts? I heard moaning... I Nikolas. Allow to run for coffee.

I look after him - cute. But following Mimi's stories about him I expected to see something... How easy for them to portray us, the artists, as idiots...

...Here appeared Mimi. When she saw me ("Did not expect!"), and even in company of Nicholas, she played amazement:

- What's going on here?

I tell. Again, doorbell rings. Big Nose Joan came. Her face shines: her husband died!! Now - litigation over the estate, but it's not so boring. Mimi, distorting, recounts my Aveyron story. Duo Mimi & Joan:

- It must be some misunderstanding, because he (Nikolas) – has beautiful blue eyes, well, just like a child...

And other nonsense.

("Eh, you bitches...")

Nicholas goes to the basement to take crutches for me, and calls a taxi to the «Hôtel-Dieu» - to a hospital for the poor.

... Hôtel-Dieu: I am sitting waiting for my turn to the surgeon. I see: from the entrance to the hall floats Madalina. Closer:

- Ninochka! What happened? Mimi said Victor...

I told her in English, Nikolas translates. Yet she's the journalist, perhaps, knows how to return my art works?

- ... threatened that if I turn to the police, he will say that I have been doing here in prostitution, and to me as a foreigner will only get worse.

- What do you mean! In France women are not punished for prostitution! Here I am, for example...

Keeps silent... Sees the young Assist (security man? Policeman? Nurse?), walking to the door. To me - in a whisper:

- Miam-miam *... (* delicious...- Fr.)

Disappeared...

Lucille took me from Mimi. It was just the last week of month, and I paid for a month.

- Good luck. I do not owe you, Mimi?

("Hope to not meet you in century.")

- No, everything is okay.

("Yeah, u-hu, like okay.")

I said goodbye to Nicholas - he collected his works back to Brittany. A friend of Lucille, the same Solange that can give for rent a small room, returned to Paris, need to wait for her arrival, and now we are at Lucille's... I see new works in the style of "spray" - author is preparing for the exhibition in the same gallery, two blocks from her house, the gallery what is not for foreigners. Now Lucille wants to send an Email to a Russian guy, or rather "ex", she would tell him that my Aveyron' story, ask his advice - what's his name? Oh, remembered, Valery - and thus she hopes reconnect... He was such a gentle...

("How is it in French!")

- Write if you want ("to return your ex-"). And then, Lucille, may you let me send one Email? I know one woman whose son is a police officer in Paris...

- Well, you'll write, you'll send your Email, then, after me.

"Dear Francine!

So I need your help...

The doorbell rings – I'll finish the letter later. Solange: stately, green-eyed, with a red mane to the waist. Without further ado she takes my belongings and carries into her car:

- Go.

~

…Mom's grave was overgrown with red poppies. And all around - green grass…

I wake up. I am at Solange', on a green bed. Or rather, on a half-bed: rest of space of the bed and the room up to the window – occupied, cluttered, filled up. Window - a guess, somewhere behind the glove deposits. I want to see what kind of a book on the shelf a meter away from my bed, but I cannot overcome the barrier of the old chair between us. (There is another room where impossible to enter.) Solange obsessed with the collection and storage, her own bedroom is also more like a storage chamber than the bedchamber. Perhaps it is in the French? Though the rest of her a rare spiritual simplicity woman. Now she's sleeping. Soon wakes up, today she has to be somewhere at two p.m., somewhere to sell pre-Christmas toys, and we will have breakfast at the kitchen half-table.

~

…Evening. Solange and I drink red wine. "Oh, do not in the fridge! It's the *red yet…*" Solange versed in wines, teaching me how to store and how to drink properly, and generally gives good advices on the house works, and in the field of etiquette. She disliked New York: "New York City - an epidemic of ambition" (Well, maybe it is.) "And Paris?" - I ask. "Paris..." (think). "... The city of love?" – I suggest. He laughs: "Well, yes. And from it is our loneliness". We laugh together.

- You know what? – says Solange. - I have an idea: let you completely recover, we will go to the village when this one... will have some "customer"... Climb into his house and steal your art works!

- What do you mean! - I'm scared. - Not a good idea! Then we'll go to jail for penetration.

It has been pretty days, and I can move around - with crutches, true, but I can. Tomorrow - the police. Lucille volunteered to walk me there to translate from English into French, and from French into English.

... Phone call from Madalina, to home phone of Solange, she got Solange's number from Lucille - I have a phone no longer, my phone stayed on the Aveyron road; Madalina said that she is outraged by what happened; that she broke up with Mimi, and that I need to spend the night with her, Madalina: to get from her some important instructions to the police on the eve of the campaign. She convinced me.

In the evening I'm in the "La Courneuve» * (* La Courneuve, Paris borough) have reached the place. Madalina beckons to her computer:

- Look, Ninochka, what I wrote to Victor. He wants to meet me, he likes me, and I – well, look what I said!

Victor to Madalina:

«Puis-je vous voir?» (Can I see you?)

Madalina - to Victor:

«Je n'aime pas les hommes violents» (I do not like the cruel men.)

I shrug: he seems to have a sense of impunity. Or he wants to inquire of me through Madalina?

- What are the instructions you give me...

- Ah, Ninochka, your "you"...

- What did you want to tell me, Madalina? What advice? Something important for police...

- A-a, Ninochka, I have prepared for you dress, in which you will go to the police.

- What dress? I think I dressed decently. Fine.

- Ninochka! Do not forget that in the police men are working. You're dressed, but not enough sexy. Here, look, this dress. I liked it and I bought it, but it's too small for me. You, Ninochka, with your figure, just right! Well, take, and then return to me back, I hope to lose weight. Dress, dress, look! Oh! Très bien! Très très bien!!

The dress - made of gray fabric with sequins and irregular in length skirt just above the knees. My white blouse and black skirt - drastically put in a plastic bag.

- You will go tomorrow in this!

("To hell with it. In the end, what's the difference...")

Her phone rings: someone needs "Romanian massage." ...Muted conversation-arrangement.

- You can go to bed to sleep, Ninochka, I will lay on the couch, and I...

And runs to the bathroom – to paint her eyes, comb hair, or rather to dissolve her gray hair on her shoulders (does not interfere with the massage?) ...Throws in her mouth a handful of some spices - to chew on, get rid of the bad smell, the teeth are not well, ache:

- ...I'll come back in two (showing two fingers) hours.

She will come at two in the morning. (I did not dare to look how she sleeping, I mean with open eyes or...)

In the morning in addition to the wacky gray dress with sequins, she gives me the bracelet the one from the African she removes from her hand and puts it on my hand. Well, that's ...I would take it out from my hand unnoticed on the road or... She curls my hair and makes "fleece" a la Brigitte Bardot: "Très bien!" Then she dresses on herself black dress with the very low-cut and goes with me, under the pretext "for the company".

At Metro Lucille waiting:

- Lol! What a look...

The police station in the area of Mimi, that is, in the area of the studio "R.A.", because here began the story. We enter. Sit. Wait. The office door opens. ...On the threshold is the dazzling beauty blond - police:

- Come on. You and... Who the translator? You (Lucille). And you (Madalina) free. (It sounded so: «Entrez, qui est traducteur? Vous? (Lucille) Mais vous (Madalina) sortir»)

Lucille and I come in - I'm leaning on crutches, pulling off on the move the bracelet: my appearance already quite ridiculous.

〰

"... But it seems that the police not in a hurry to help non-Frenches. Yes, and Lucille made emphasis on the fact that my physical injuries, while I - all I wanted was to return to my works, that is, return stolen. Lucille, being obsessed with love stories - on the muzhiki* (*simple men) in other words, Russian words - I think the investigator presented Aveyron' history as a case with ami abusif, that is violent boyfriend. Remembering that she had a Russian friend, who with her for a long time does not talk, does not answer, she wrote him Email with a description of what happened to me and requested to respond and advise (what?) - So she wanted this way to return the Russian guy. What can I say?

Oh, playful, toy French soul!

Well, well, enough about that. I am glad that your hand has healed and that Mitya so... Everything will be fine."

~

Email – respond from Francine:

"Good day, my dear!

I'm so glad to hear from you. I'm fine, recently celebrated the birthday of my granddaughter, Evelyn - 4 years old! There were a lot of visitors. You know, we, the

French, are very strong family ties! I wish you a happy return to New York.

Kiss you, my dear.

Francine."

Not a word in reply to my request. ("... Strong family ties...")

Madalina phoned, to invite... to Mimi for tea. What? Tea with Mimi? That's all I lacked. «Merci» Thank you, unfortunately I cannot.

❧

... African lady, whom Solange works for (selling souvenirs and trinkets) – has as much as three husbands. One is in Africa, and the other lives in the suburbs of Paris, and the third - in Belgium. And this emancipated Woman of the East, or rather of the Southern Hemisphere, told Solange to fetch her for a few days in Belgium, to the third husband. (For Solange rented hotel room.)

I, after seeing Solange, was going to make a dinner.

A phone call: Madalina, cartoon voice again:

- Ninochka! I have good news! I want to publish book of poetry, Romanian poetry, and thou shalt be illustrating. I've already reached an agreement with the publisher... with the lady publisher. We organize sorority. You will then need to move to my place, you might pay half of my rent. Later... And now come here, I'll show you the book. Come with an overnight stay, take everything for signing the contract, passport, etc., tomorrow meet with the publisher and negotiate... Waiting at nine in the evening. Nine zero zero. See you soon, a bien tôt...

Wow... Yet Madalina is a good person, though strange. Very strange, but... human... Illustrating Romanian poetry! This is... What an unexpected twist! Romanian poetry... In general, in all poetry including Romanian should be an image of a rose. Seven o'clock. There is still time. Inspiration... Watercolor is ready: a huge red rose, which a woman like Madalina hugging: black laughing eyes without eyelids, like a doll; light (gray) hair dissolved on her shoulders... Her hands were pierced a rose, they passed through, as if wearing a flower, having covered it as a towel after shower... More watercolors: circle. Just circle. Inside, within a circle - bushes of strawberries - berries, leaves, flowers... Oops, half of the eighth. I'm going to. In the bag - a bank card, phone, wallet, phone book, diary, sketches, passport... close the door - keys in the bag. Eight o'clock, I hasten to hobble to the subway, getting dark.

... La Courneuve. Then a couple of stops on the tram... I go to the house of Madalina. In front of me three teenagers in hoods, turn right, cross the road and - the path through some triangular garden with stunted trees... ("Nine in the evening. Do you know where your children are?" American TV advertising.) I turn left. I come to the entrance, press the bell to her apartment... does not open. Does not hear? Press more, and more... Someone is touching the back of my shoulder - apparently, someone wants to open the door with his key. I turned around - I see hooded faces of three teenage Africans, who silently, all in silence, rip the bag off my shoulder...

- A-aaaaaaa!!!

On my cries did not open any window.

I do not just give the bag, pull the handle off, I fall on the stone porch, getting a kick in my teeth, and they run away into the darkness to the right. Silently. Oh. Something sticky on the back of the head: blood. I hasten to an Arab shop, thank God, it's still open. Arabs wipe the blood on my head, on the back of my head, cauterize the wound. Call the police. Police we had to wait a long time, forty-five minutes.

... At the police station 2am. Police engaged in some kind of couple who have been robbed - someone stole their car.

... 2:30. The young officer beckons me to say: if I give him 150 euros, he will help me enter into the entrance of Madalina's house. He's accompanying his words with drawings: "150E". What is "150E", look, I have empty hands, but that's one glove and the other carried away with the bag. And why do I access Madalina! I actually went to her I actually went to her on a business trip... "Do you have someone else's, Paris phone?" Lucille. Well, how well I remember. (Phone book in the bag, the bag was taken away.) Call... Lucille: "Call a taxi, I'll pay." Taxi... Arrive... Lucille meets near her house, pays the price with the taxi driver. In house she lays me on the floor, right under the canvas a la Pollock - in her bedroom is boyfriend, asleep. "Get down here... Yes, there on the table, you'll see 70 Euro. You need these days. You may give when you can."

...Walking in La Courneuve police and requesting to take from me a list documents and things which gone with the silent Africans do not have success. They, the policemen, have to celebrate some French holidays, which they cannot ignore. "Come back later on". And Madalina – what's with Madalina? Do not return phone calls.

... Finally, I succeeded to block my bank card. Meanwhile, reported online, someone has already tried to buy something using my passport data - not knowing how to name the bank (did not have time?), and decided that all the banks in America are called "Bank of America"... Such situation...

US Embassy: in the hall of the Embassy - crowd of victims in Paris, robbed, beaten, roofless, they settled on the sofa, on the floor, on the chairs... Children, women... Eh, Paris, Paris... ...Days in efforts to restore my ID. Window №... recommended me ask my daughter for an e-ticket to New York. "-?" Oh, no, no... she had enough... Besides, we live in different states at different rates... ... different forms of economy... It is not up to me. It is better to... Better in... (What?)

For a while I kept at the head of my bed the parting words by my favorite philosopher D. Arundel, something like this (I took off from the wall, but remember): "... All around you may crumble – buildings, relations, your friends, relatives, the closest ones will turn away from you... But if you tell yourself: "All is fine" and go ahead - everything will be fine..."

So I have all come true in the first part of those parting words: family and closest, including daughter turned away from me; home is gone long ago, collapsed many, actually collapsed, crumbled all hopes. But only the latest - *allisfine* does not work. Well, go ahead. That is, backwards. Paris - New York. (After all, I got help with the ticket...) All the way I am going to think: what is with my watercolors? On the "flea-market" whether next to toy cars, or in the house of a Russian collector of Naivism? Idiotism... What happened to Madalina? To calls from Lucille and Solange she did not answer...

∽

Before my departure from Paris I came to the Jardin Luxembourg, and of course, I made a couple of watercolors. Petunias in the wonderful vase were replaced by chrysanthemum, also purple, but different shades of purple and all the same dark purple. Yet the "back-ground" is block buildings, and trees in the distance beyond the garden, not pleasing the eye by green dome, but rather saddened by some shabbiness and nakedness. Leaving, I made a circle along the sculpture gallery, stood a long time near the George Sand stone:

"How you lived, a Great Woman, how you created in Your Century?..."

And then, suddenly - from Victor shameless email:

«C›est toi je l›ai vole» (It is you who have robbed me.)

- ? What else is for nonsense!

After all this, if is it worth to take seriously the so-called French system of justice and related French systems! Throw to the devil's mother all these protocols, and even X-rays - to recover in spite of them!!!

... And here I am in New York.

Train, the train "B". Entry and exit people with troubled fates, and they seem to give me energy and courage to live on.

*...I came to a half-destroyed house in which **S.** lived. I began to try, and was able to collect something, to restore - the walls, floor, seats... There's a lovely woman who introduced herself as his sister Kunka. (Truth, I remember, he told me, that he has sister Kunka). I told her: "To see him and to die".*

In fact, to see him, and then to die...

I woke up in a dorm on the bed by the window.

"... You do not worry about me, Olesya. All the bad is behind. All the documents from the hospital and the police services answers, I simply threw in the trash. To spite of fate and circumstances, I recovered by memory most of my stolen works, some get even better! Only, however, I do not participate in exhibitions... yet. I'm going to the post office - send to you earrings...

December in New York

In Tompkin square, I met Michelle - the very Michelle, who showed the film about unrequited love, with girl walking with her friend near the shoe store. Michelle kept on a leash a cute red-haired dog.

- Michelle! Hello! Glad to see you!

- I, too, hello! For a long time in Paris? Why a cane?

- Oh, it's... From Paris with Love.

- What? Ha ha ha... Oh, I remember, there once I met Madalina in the metro, so she was for some reason, boasted to me that slept with an African teenager. ...In my opinion, she is crazy.

- True? I, too, heard, she talked about it... It's probably the climax... menopausal hot flushes. And my works were stolen... That handyman - friend of Mimi... all watercolors... And the-en...

- Oh, oh... How?! I do not understand how you could communicate with him, I did not like him at once, and in general they are all there... except for Guillaume. How is he?

- Unfortunately, he is not there, it seems, has returned to his Normandy. ("By the way, if all people are beautiful?") And how are you, Michelle? What movie you shot?

- Nothing, I sit here with the dog - owners away, asked to look. Dog-sitting. For 10 bucks a day. You have Email?

- Of course. Here. Poka* (*bye-Rus.). Good-bye.

- Poka. Good-bye.

NY. December also

The bill came from the hospital Hôtel-Dieu, 80 Euros, or $120, I paid inadvertently twice that is, the requirement to pay came again, and I, afraid that my previous check was lost on the road, sent anew $120. Neither one of the two checks was lost, but to return the overpayment, trop-payé, the Hôtel-Dieu will not.

And then - Email, Email from gray Romanian Madalina. When I saw her name, I was delighted: alive! - But...

«Ecoute, envoyez-moi deux mille Euro.

... Je te répète tes responsabilités et qu'est-ce que tu as à payer: mon soutien pour t'accompagner à l'hôpital et à la police était soumis aux conditions: 100 euros par jours. Tu connais compter, n'est-ce pas? Le totale: 500 euros..."

("Hey, send me two thousand Euro.

... I repeat your duties and what you have to pay: my support, to accompany you to the hospital and the police under the terms: 100 euros per day. You know the score, right? Total: 500 euros..."

Next - even some fictitious services to me – the gray with sequins sexy dress and bracelet made of adhesive tape from the African; total rental... 2000, two thousand Euro. Not a word about the African teenagers. Does not know... Does not know? Where she was?)

Such flushes! Perhaps the message was for me the biggest shock. I consider her, if not a friend, then at least a native human... Human...

∽

"Good afternoon, Nina!

Bonjour!

It's me, Solange. Hello from Lucille also. She is in trouble: fired. During her boss' absence for vacation she decided to arrange her personal exhibition in his office, exhibition and sale. Someone told to boss, and she was fired. Well, she will - you know her - survive. Survive. She gets out of the situation. She relies on show at some gallery near her home. Though you never know...

O, I want to show you, Nina, a funny ad I saw, passing by the monastery of Mimi:

"**Décembre -2009 Paris. Dans le «RA » Galerie -
Exposition et
vente aquarelles de l'artiste américaine Nina C.
- Seuls 22 œuvres. L'exposition se ouvre
15 décembre 19 heures.**"

("December -2009 Paris. The Gallery "R. A. "-
Exhibition and
Sale watercolors of American artist Nina C.
- A total of 22 works. The exhibition opens
December 15, 19 hours.")

What do you think?"

- Hmm... 22... Where else 3?

IV

....

ALL NIGHT WAS RAIN

No matter how much talk about sad,
No matter how often contemplate on the ends and
beginnings,
Yet, I dare to think,
What you only fifteen years old.
So I would like to
So you fell in love with the common man,
Who loves the earth and the sky
More than rhymed and unrhymed speech about the
land and the sky
(Alexander Blok, "When you stand in my way...")

"The whole night was rain…"

"That's how I will call my next story. Or so I'll start…"

With that thought, I wake up.

In fact, it turns out, it was not and is not raining, and it was and is the traffic noise outside. To come and see… Came up.

Look.

Remember…

~

May 2013

… I came, flew to Moscow to publish a book for the "Russian Booker", to publish and deliver, by my own hands to carry to Booker - application and the book in six copies: then they will not be able to say "not received" and blame the postal service, as they did previously. Of course, I remember Anna Akhmatova said: "They reward themselves". But the prizes were six, even if the winner would be one of "friends" and will get a million, let them! I might be among the other five, and five thousand is enough to make a difference, five thousand dollars is enough to buy an old, even very, very old house… in Bulgaria. The hopes were fueled by the presence of my own illustrations to the text. After all, I'm still an artist! Though not participate in exhibitions... yet.

Plot: *Man and Woman, destined for each other, finally meet in advanced age.*

I went to the JFK * (* the airport in New York) with a sense of emptiness and could not remember in Moscow no place that I would like to visit.

Arrived at May 9 - Victory Day

In New York, was a terrible cold, so I was dressed in a winter long black coat, and in Moscow - a terrible heat, and black coat on me, or rather, I in black and long coat looked ridiculous, but it was not possible and no place to change clothes in the summer dress. I went in search of the hostel, crossing the Bolshoi Theatre Square. There was crowded - gathered survivors of the war; on a small open area was the concert stage: female soprano singing songs of the war years; adolescents and young people came to the elderly and handed them flowers - roses, carnations. It was touching. This was beautiful.

I in my black coat walked through the crowd of perky people, and recalled the very first Victory Day in Siberia: red and pink scarves like banners on the roofs of the village barns... Back to the village returned alive only three men: Uncle Zahar returned one-legged,

Uncle Vasya M. came on foot from Berlin carrying the trophy embroidered towels in a bag; Uncle Daniel – with German postcards: birds, beautiful colored birds, he them (the postcards) hung in the house of his mother - aunt Sophia, in the kitchen at the dinner table. I was looking any occasion to visit Aunt Sophia to look at them again and again...

...Finally, found, settled in the hostel called "Godzilla". I did not see that image in movie and the movie is not seen. I saw the picture on the wall of the hostel Godzilla, then - the owner of the hostel - by the way, an American looking exactly like wall paintings, and this was enough... Again went I to the center on Pushkin Square. Square was empty from the veterans and were only screens with congratulations.

I sat down on the bench with two old ladies, one with pink bow, the other which closer to me - even without. The old woman with a pink bow says to another that close to me:

- ... You what, do not you know who is Agnes Barto *? (* Agnes Barto - children's poet) What are you, educate your children ("grandchildren" - I corrected mentally) without her poems?! How to...

Another, that close to me:

- Yes, without Agnes Barto.

- What are they listening to? Rock music?

- Yes, to rock music. Children ("grandchildren" - again I corrected mentally) need to know the rhythm.

The new generation of old ladies... I slowly pinched of bread from the loaf what I bought on the road and gave the pigeons. They were a few - hungry and timid... I remembered my and my mother's futile attempts to find the burial place of my father, "Missing", but rather, killed near Rzhev...

I went back.

Waking up the next day, I did not find the rest of my bread: someone took it and ate it. Bon Appetit. I had to settle for coffee, imported from New York and brewed here. But from the kitchen window I heard Rooster "Ku-ka-re-kuu!" – someone holding a rooster at this bird? It is great, it is so great for the city. However, it could be Clock on the building of Puppet Theatre Obraztsov, because the theater just across the street, that is, the ring, the Sadovoe...

And in the evening - from the same kitchen window - wonderful polyphonic singing: it seems, in the cafe at the bottom of the building, Georgian ensemble singing. There were performed four songs, four charming Georgian songs.

∾

"Крутится, вертится дворник с метлой"

"Spinning, spinning janitor with a broom..."

(paraphrase of Russian pop-song "Blue Ball" from movie "Youth of Maxim")

Moscow streets are clean. But for some reason this does not suit the Asian street cleaners, a huge number of them rushing around every corner of the capital with a broom in hand. I see: a young Asian man, a Tajik or Uzbek with a mini-scythe in his hands, cuts at the root of red poppies on a lawn near the monument to Mayakovsky, then to plant on this place other flowers, more modest, not poppies, not red. (Just like in humans...) I turned into an alley called before "Yuzhinsky", where I had once lived... and where was briefly married to the father of my daughter, God rest his soul... Things changed, impossible to recognize. It seems that all the tenants were evicted, and now everything is entirely business area. So I came to Patriarch Ponds. Out of habit, I look around, puzzling, "By what way passed the tram, where the notorious Anna spilled sunflower oil on which Misha Berlioz slipped; where his severed head rolled? * "(*" Master and Margarita "by Mikhail Bulgakov) Surely someone else comes here with the same puzzle, but meanwhile, it's all or almost all invented not quite healthy imagination of not too humane author. Along Malaya Bronnaia I reached his dwelling. Once, many years ago, fans of this work and its author - mostly teenagers, and among them my daughter - came to worship at the entrance, where the writer lived. Then police broke them up, and now, realizing finally that of worship possible to have a profit, ie profit, city officials and enthusiasts emptied and equipped the historic dwelling under the house-museum with an impressive entrance fee, entrance and surrounding wall decorated by grapffiti illustration - scenes from the novel.

∿

May 11, Saturday

This is only second day of the weekend, a total number of them is four, and for publishers, too. Such date for the arrival I have chosen! To live up to Monday!

...I go down from the bottom shelf of hostel bunk-bed. Room mixed, ie mixed for sleeping both sexes, all of us 12, twelve, most - students, tourists. The main "action" person is a tall blond German who leads every night to his bed another girl. «Tonight I'm gonna fuck her» - he announces, and then merged with her in his arms, until morning creaks by his bottom shelf by the window. All roommates tolerate, perhaps asleep. And this is days of Victory over...

Shower is alright, but the toilet... It is also "mixed", as a bedroom, so, fearing that "everything can be heard," ... the first thing in the morning I do - go to the nearest McDonald's that on Tverskaya. It is close to the places where I had once lived (and where...), only instead of "Mac" cafe was cafe "Lira", where was played in the evenings dance music; passing by the windows of the cafe, you could see the singer - maiden with thickly powdered face; locals and passers-by called her "Singing Powder Compact." What happened to her? Perhaps, it's the short-haired woman with a mop in hand, frown glance escorting to the toilet cabine... Now passed to the door - I wash my hands - looked back... Phew!

Now I can buy their coffee.

Smiling waiters mostly Asians, as well as diligent janitors on the streets of the capital. I am leaving with a coffee to the table. The man at the next table looks closely, it seems, is trying to remember me. In vain:

I am the one whom no one remembers.

12 May, Sunday Morning

… Sliding-crawled down.

McDonald's

Yesterday I made several successive attempts to request online the place of burial of my father. Responses were standard, "do not know", "we have no information", and so on. And so all the time, that is all life. Poor Mama. So she died without having the information.

- Coffee, please.

I can still afford potatoes "a peasant". They make tasty, do not leave the peel like in the US McDonald's, but cleaned and baked...

- Woman! There is occupied!

Strange, now here appeal to the lady in Russia: not the "Madame", not a "lady", not "senora", not a "miss" or even "comrade", but "woman" - as well as in the gynecology office...

- Excuse me.

I go to another table.

... I suddenly realized what I will do for the soul: go to the Lefortovo Val, 7/6, that is, the house of our former dormitories – my and his, **S.'** It is a pity that we are scattered, and that can not return. From this is my obsession in recent years - a house in Bulgaria that is a house where he returned to, where I can breathe the same air with him.

...I came. First by metro to station "Bauman" then walking along the tram route and passing Bauman Park. I came, I learned, here it is: Lefortovo Val, 7/6. However, the buildings-dorms for the other faculties were removed, demolished, and only ours (his and mine) left - the red building at Lefortovsky Val, 7/6.

But beneath the arch that separated our porches, are no longer entrance in the student cafeteria, it's gone, the house is fenced, no chance to come closer to his window... I went around the corner to a nearby yard, and took a photo of our windows - mine, his, from the side. On the way back - the store, the same old shop where I used to buy sweets. ...Victory Day' parade: I was assigned to go in the column. We walked from the building of the Institute of Krasnokazarmennaya. When reached angle Krasnokazarmennaya with Lefortovo Val, I could not resist the temptation to slip out of the ranks of the column; ran to the store, bought a cake and something sweet, a lot of sweet... To the column I did not returned.

... I stopped by in the store and bought prianik* (*honey cake), eaten on the move, going along Krasnokazarmennaya to the building of the institute. Came. The building did not disappoint me: the same beautiful and majestic, with a poster - Congratulations on the Victory Day. I photographed. Now went back to the station "Baumanskaya" and mentally asked forgiveness from **S**. - I do not know what for apologized, walked, and imagined: here we are with him as some years ago, walk side by side, step by step; I am in pink dress of stiff fabric, "Taffeta", he is in blue shirt; I press to my chest his gift - plastic toy souvenir "roly-poly" which later I hurled to his face when I saw ("cought") him with another woman, or rather, a woman, unlike me - ignorant girl. One would not notice, just step aside, to remain silent, to wait. But this tactic is not for young age.

Well, now going back to Metro by foot. Bauman Park. Greens, greens… Wooden house - public toilet, sloped floor with a hole inside for excrementing, stench, fear to fall down into hole – all the same as many years ago. Left, remembering:

…He stopped near our table where my Bulgarian girlfriend Blazhka and I finishing our lunch. He says to Blazhka:

"And tomorrow is my birthday…"

(He says it in Russian, so, what he says must be addressed to me.)

That was February 18th - Day of his appearance for me, and it means, his birthday is February 19th.

…Finally, reached hostel, fell asleep like dead.

May 13th. Monday McDonalds

Coffee… Publishing house

Now I'm sitting expecting for an editor. I arrived here for this, for sitting expecting for an editor. My thoughts like billows: tide, low tide, tide, low tide, etc., and I forgot what I thought about… A-a, that's what about: I might sit here for long time. But my longtime practice of expectations will help me sit motionless for long, for hours.

...My expectations fulfilled. She came. The editor – beauty! Breathtaking! (Good I sit.) Picture "Ava Gardner revisited" She offered me a tea, I did not resist. ...Writes me recommendation for the "Booker", and I have bring it to the address of "Booker".

May 14th – Tuesday, May 15th – Wednesday

"But I am going, walking through Moscow

And I would walk much more else..."

Interesting, how "much more else" I would walk? In New York I used to walk by foot (from economy) from two hundred to four hundred blocks, there was walking by straight line, but here – along the curve, that is the "ring" (Sadovoe). At first day of walking, by foot from economy, I returned back to hostel with horrible aches in legs. Now – I can, I walk. That "Booker» is in such a remote place, probably for to not everyone could reach. (Winners of the "Booker" must be those who are quick and good walkers?) I walked in different directions from "Smolenskaya", that was said "in direction of "naberezhnaya"* (*embankment), but which "naberezhnaya"? Here are many... Finally, found, thanks to the man with the dog in one of the back yards. In a little room of "Booker" sat a sad woman. She accepted the application with a somber face: "Well." Now I have to annoy publisher asking make the book ready for Booker until June 14 (author's copies promised to June 20), this deadline.

Beauty-editor, handing me the application, said by the way, that Svetlana is searching for me.

...That was in New York. Street books seller came to me and asked if I can read Russian.

"Yes."

"Then take these books, seems to me, they are in Russian."

The books were indeed in Russian, one by B.Akunin, I read it and gave to my acquaintance, another book – book of poetry by Svetlana; it, I mean the book I left and keep for myself. Such nice poetry, unusually, untypically nice, delightful... I saw her e-mail address, wrote her, and we began contact. Later she published two more books of poetry and sent to me in New York. Now I am in Moscow, and Svetlana wants to meet me. We agreed: twelve o'clock (midday), near Pushkin' monument. For meeting I decided to wear shoes with highest platform, thinking: anyway, to communicate with her I would look up: Svetlana seemed tall girl. I came to place of meeting half hour earlier. Looked some shadowy place - sun was burning. On the bench from left burning heat. Went to right, passing monument, or rather flowers near monument, turned back: along Tverskaya walked a fragile girl with fair hair in green dress; her face seemed to me familiar from somewhere... From past time, but when?.. Here she smiled, waved me by hand... Closer:

- I recognized you at first sight!

That was Svetlana, in shoes on highest hills, and we were the same heights.

- Where we'll go?

- "Winzavod"!* (*Wine factory) I wanted so much to visit that Gallery, I read about it a lot. We wandered for while in areas of Kursky Vokzal* (*railroad station). Finally, came, found: factories buildings and constructions; indeed, the wine factory.

In a labyrinth of those constructions – some shows with intriguing names. We selected solo show of painting - it's simplier, and cheaper, although actually the sum is expressive, 150 rubles, in dollars - $5. In New York visiting of galleries are free, and to the opening receptions half of New Yorkers hurry for free wine and snacks – cheese, chips and so on. ...Went down into basement – space, hall. Along the walls – fifteen canvases, dirty-grey-lilac color. Minimalism? Marasmus? Svetlana smiled absently to me, I smiled guilty to her: yet, she paid! To us in basement came down a young girl, possible "guide" or "critic", and started talk us in fancy words about how the author of canvases worked over that exposition two years, and what he "kept in mind"...

We left without knowing what he kept in mind.

Kept silent...

- Actually, in New York galleries the expositions are the same absurd. Visitors crowd there only at opening days – you may guess why.

- Why?

- Because of free wine and snacks.

- Aaa...

- Some times ago I was member of Committee on Malaya Grusinskaya... That was the union of independent artists. Now there is no union anymore. Since then, I can see, there happened hairpin bend, or, rather deadend in creative genre of Russian 2000s...

- A-aa... And where we go now?

- If you did not tired with me...

- No, no, what are you....

- Then maybe, "Garage"? Gorky Park (of Culture...)

We went by foot. The weather was wonderful: dry, warm. In and near undergroung crossings we saw real may flowers for sale. On Old Arbat – multiplicity of art or para-art pieces-souvenirs: pictured mayflowers, poppies, forge-me-not, bluebells and cupolas, faces, kitties, doggies; everything here calls: "Buy me!" and "I can draw you?"

Although the artists entered the fashion photo-realism, and forms of the depicted objects are absolutely accurate, - seriously, that is by soul, can be perceived only a few (among them are the work of a pair of artists represented by initials, asking the name would be inappropriate, because we are not buyers) the immediacy of expression seems lost.

We reached, came in the Gorky Park of Culture. Sat on the grass in the shade of some trees, Svetlana said that she had a gift for me from her husband: a bottle of balsam from Veliky Novgorod; we opened a bottle of balsam from Veliky Novgorod, made a sip for a meeting. Repeat did not dare, besides it is forbidden - to drink alcohol in a public place. We talked about our affairs…

FIRST LOVE

We sat in the park,
On the grassy meadow
Breathing aromas of late spring.
We - different people,

Whole life is between us...
God knows why
And for whom we are needed.

You told me about
Your first feeling,
In the name of what
You passed all roads.
To live by first love
Is not art, but a feat of
mysterious Russian soul.

God knows why
And who needs it,
to cherish
Such strange heritage
as Love,
to drink everyday by mugs, Memory,
Without torment
to live

(Svetlana Oleinik, "First Love")

We stood up – and in "Garage". Full immediacy we found while visiting "Garage". The exhibition name was "Museum of all Exhibition #5". We read on prospect: the founder of Museum, Englishman James Brett, he also director of Museum, displaying non-traditional art and creations by artists-self taught in whole world. Last summer James made trip over Russian towns in search of works by unknown artists, and now, as result of that colossal work – exhibition of fifty unknown unrecognized Russian contemporary artists. Among them – naivists, self taught, autists, mentally sick, prisoners, homeless, disabled; artists creating in difficult situations, who not tied by frames of traditions and not hoping for profit, working in different styles and different by available technics.

A strongest impression made on us creative work by "Old Man B.U.Kashkin", who lived and died in Irkutsk in 2005 at the age of 65 years: on the three planes, one of which - a tray - the theme of food. On the tray - the following dishes: "eda1", "eda*(*food) 2", "eda3" and coarsely written: "Come let us overeat and do not let us starve" On the second plane (canvas?) - Boundless water surface - whether the sea, or ocean; ship passing the Statue of Liberty; a ship flying with the banner "Soon we will ochen food"; and airplane. The third work - "And will the food." It seems that the author's theme speaks for itself... It's to me, who grew up in a Siberian village, so familiar...

(That will be bitter disappointment will soon to learn (Ivanov, "Ёburg"), that "B.U.Kashkin" - Eugene Malakhin last successful engineer who for instance by Paul Gauguin, one day decided to move into the world of "La Boheme": second marriage - though in the city and not on the island of Haiti, the work as janitor, paintings, inferior Gogen's on skill, but surpassing by audacity self-expression, eccentric clothing and a swarm of fans, fans... And he died, as he lived, in Yekaterinburg, not in Irkutsk.)

...The whole wall by unusual graphic by Vasily Romanenkov from Dubrovka from Smolensk region. Vasily grew up in a family of workers of the funeral service, according to the organizers of the exhibition, as we read. His uncles did tombstones, and thus, for Vasily at an early age the border between life and death was blurred. It is remarkable and sad that he died on the opening day. Near some of his works you have to stand for while and you need to see. It is creativity "Revival of undervalued architecture of the Russian spirit" - a figure in profile; resembling the Egyptian; temples; decorations... Work, where lots of architectural objects, scenes, and in the middle of a tiny square, barely fit the word "life". The professionalism of performance seems much higher, more serious than B.U.Kashkin.

On the next wall - watercolors by Peter Polishchuk, and that's his story, told by a cute girl Oksana - the guard of the exhibition: Peter as child lost his parents, grew up in an orphanage; reaching military age sent to serve in the navy, on the submarine. His submarine was sunk in the Barents Sea, and when the submarine was taken upward from the sea, there were five dead, and only one, Peter, survived. Peter was discharged, has experienced a concussion, he began to draw. Tried to enter the Union of Artists - was rejected. Still, he was grateful to jury of Union for the advice "work on marine theme". True, on the second calling he was again rejected, but he keeps faithful to his theme. His watercolors - it is water, the aqua-blue, then dark green, then red from the stream coming from below, from the water; the water and submarine, and above all this - sad Face.

...Huge in length, canvas of a young artist from St. Petersburg Mikhail Mirkin "UFO, landing". Did he (author) imagine or have seen the landing? I have seen for a long time... but not so close up... it was...

And there was Vladimir Zoroastrov from Astrakhan - painted in a surprising manner, delicate by color oil/canvas religious subjects: the priest, to condemn and/or giving advice; Baptism - dive with a flying dove carrying a flower; a dive again in the presence of the three; Entombment, evidenced by monkeys... Woman breastfeeding a baby and sucking a pacifier:

"Love-Mashka-FOOL"

Different ones Fifty... I remembered the "Monument" of A.Pushkin as a spiritual testament. It turns out, Brett followed the precepts of the great poet's: be merciful to men trapped in difficult conditions, who fell, but keep devotion to creativity. Oksana said that "The Museum of all" functioning not only as an exhibition Constitution, but also as an archive. So creativity of these artists will remain in history? Great! Just wonderful and rightly so. Svetlana was gone, it was time to be with her baby at home, and I...

And I visit my countrywoman-Siberian, a former neighbor by the former house, that is, the former neighbor's little girl, and now Muscovite and the capital's keeper *"eeynogo" (*hers-sleng) home hearth.

- ... And he, whore- bitch fucked in the mouth, bitch... do not understand, asshole... as he takes the child, asshole... brings to the fucken Pizzerias, full of prostitutes, bitch... Misha comes in and says, shit: "Grandma, there Aunt Dina fell." Drunk, I suppose. Well, fuck, he shit do not do the child no little book to read, tell the tale, but he asshole, come, buy a beer, staring at the Tiwi and child itself, fuck (draws on the cigarette, sips beer from can.) And then he give child me to care, fucken in his mouth, and no shit. Tanya, mother-in-law his gave him twenty thousands, so he shit spent on the girls and for a beer... (Gulp from can of beer...) Well what a bitch, fuck Huh? (Decidedly dramatically) All pull from me! The rent I pay, fuck, for gas, fuck. Well then, fuck how to do not drink! (Gulp, another sip...)

After some conscientious translation and censorship - a history, her "Shining Path" synopsis: Siberia, the farm - Moscow, limit, factory, dormitory, abortion, a birth, a marriage, residence, husband, mother in law, children, grandchildren, vodka, Beer, cigarettes, retirement. Everest: tombstone entwined with artificial flowers.

- By the way, I could not go and see Yurik, his grave. Shit... Wait, I am right now...

She goes to barf - a necessary element of Russian culture of dark alleys. (And only Russian?) I absently listening, watching, silent, think:

"Why... Why did we leave our nests? What for?"

The narrator returns to the home hearth topic:

- ... And this, freak, geek, damn, look, look what he did...

She lifts up her blouse, turns by her back: terrible wounds, scabs, burns. I cry out:

- Oh, what's that?!

- Yeah, fuck, eldest, attached to my back of grilled meat, damn...

- Meat! Grilled! What for?

- Ah, dick knows. I overcook meat. Would you like some tea? Tomatoes? Eat!

Blows her nose on the floor... Then follow memories of her husband, who died last year, her visit to him in the hospital:

- ...Nurses, fucking... they say he did an enema, fucking... And I say them no enema you did, I slipped a finger into his ass, and there – all solid...

("Love?")

I am searching in her, but cannot find - the features of little girl with curly hair, who stands on a steep bank of our Siberian river: a short blue dress; downed knees... The sun shines her gold curls... I am down, scooped bucket of water, and with water - fry - fishes, by which we intend to feed our cats... Now I'm going up, while she there waiting for me; then along the path by the river she in front of me, but she...

- Well, cho*(*why-sl.) you do not eat tomatoes?

(Smokes... Into face... me.)

- Thank you thank you. I am full. I have to go.

Balsam I leave with her.

The burns on her back... Svetlana says that such scenes are standard in Moscow families. What are the causes of family scenes and wild mutual hatred - living space, this Moscow Klondike - Gold Rush, nullifies the family feeling, all the feeling at all.

It's a pity.

May 16, Thursday

Good morning, McDonald's toilet.

Coffee... Potatoes "a peasant", that is, it turns out, it is called "potato country like".

Potato country like... In Siberia is now Indian summer. In the gardens harvested potatoes. Dry, warm weather... The smell of disturbed nightshade... Acute attack of nostalgia... I ate "potato-peasant... that is countrylike" and go to the post office; to call to Siberia to the village, to Katya - former fellow-villager, by visiting Siberia we have stopped in her home before, and now I am asking whether to buy an abandoned house in the village - I saw such house when I was there; time ago there lived Uncle Vasia...

Katya - slurred and stammered (seemed handset breathed by moonshine):

- Oh, wwhat you ttalkin. C-come sstay in my house. What "house" what "buy"! Our h-houses, your and mine - two meters and a half - at ggraveyard!

Ah, well, I understood, I have to keep in mind here people do not live long.

The attack of nostalgia has disappeared.

...Publisher. Opt for pictures stock illustrations for my book from my computer.

May 17, Friday McDonalds. Toilet. Cafe and coffee. On the balcony through the glass window I see: a fat-girl with liquid pigtail, dressed in blue uniform, makes comments to the cleaner. Something she did not like. Reprimand - not audible, but you can see how he cringed in fear; and she turned and went quite an impression of power. There are such, quite an impression of power, and there are many.

Now I am in a park near the Yuri Dolgoruky monument. I bought coffee at McDonalds, though I already had coffee at home that is at the hostel – this I bought just for capacity for water for a watercolor. Water from the fountain... I hasten to capture the beauty of the plants near the monument. A man on a bench across the park looking at me closely, what I'm doing, and all what are like that. I'm drawing. *I am nobody for him, and I think it's mutual.*

...Returned to the hostel. Noon. View from Hostel window: group of young people, work in unison with their motorcycles, and now, in unison just sit around near their motorcycles, drink beer and talk - probably about motorcycles. One of them on the sidelines talking on the phone with his mistress:

- ...Bitch! Where did you go, whore...?

Su... Such... like Romeo! (Is it New Russian?)

Romeo with a bottle in hand goes back to his motorcycle.

My book is not ready.

May

Good morning, uni... McDonald's.

The book is not ready.

May 28

"November 1941.

Good afternoon, my dearest ones...

... We with our military unit located near Moscow. We (my friend and I) stand at one woman's house. She for us, Maroussia, refers like to her own sons, and from her sons from the front she does not get any news.

... All anything, but we suffer from furunkuls (blain). Painful...damp...

... Kisses to my dear baby daughter...

... And I have no address, Maroussia, yet, as soon as will be the address – I'll inform.

I remain,

Yours, loving husband and father..."

"May, 2013

Good afternoon!

How to search for information about relatives, you can come out of "search technology," posted on the website http://www.soldat.ru/doc/search.

Try to ask for help to find information on the forum at http://forum.patriotcenter.ru/ section "Soldiers of Destiny".

You should also make a request to:

1. The center Investigation and Information Society of the Red Cross, Russian Federation.

Location Centre: 103031, Moscow, st. Kuznetsky Most, 18/7; Tel.: (8-495) 921-71-75; fax: 923-45-80.

2. Central Archives of the Ministry of Defense of the Russian Federation (CAMD).

Address file: 142100, Moscow region, Podolsk, ul. Kirov, 74

tel.: (8-496) 769-96-20, (8-496) 769-90-05,

E-mail in the archive there.

3. Voenkomat the place of recruitment.

4 Archive military Medici... museum... Ministers of Defense of the Russian F... ....

Address file: 191180, St. Pete... Lazarus... f... 2... (8-812) 315-72-91.

5. Organization of graves - an... ... equ... Ministers of the Russian Federation for... perpetuate the memory of those killed in the defense of the Patriotic...

6... 7... 8... 9... 10... ... ...

Yours faithfully,

The corporation "Electronic Archive» http://www. elar.ru"

Here are standart answers which come every time, and there, at these locations, just transmit over the line to another address. How I see these employees no one of them lost relatives, no one of theirs perished.

"Falcon, my falcon, which land drank your blood, where your white bones scattered? If I had known..."

(Lullaby)

In early childhoods for us, orphans - and there have been a lot such, a lot - a fact of dead or missing relatives was an unavoidable reality, and "burial place" was the front, the war...

Growing up, we somehow sharper feel their physical absence.

My father was 27. My father is 27.

June 2nd Sunday

They promised next week make six control copies for "Booker" unlaminated, I will go for 4 days in Sofia, for the meeting with the agent for the sale of the property: to meet, to look; I think when I get back, the book will be ready, and will still not too late for the Booker. Short of money, and little chance to buy this property, it is a house in the Bulgarian countryside, but to look - visit on the ground S. Moscow-Sofia... Sofia-Moscow... Moscow-New York. And after 3 months I will be crying from happiness because sixth place of Booker Prize.

Svetlana says: "Why is the 6th? You need to tune to the first place. The first place!" But I can not tune to the first place. First place can turn to me a heart attack, but I need to keep my health.

Sofia! Soon I will see Sophia... I feel already as though one leg in Sofia. I am going to the station, to know, to buy a ticket.

When I was walking by the platform towards my last vagon, I saw a young man who asked wistfully, how to get by train to Konotop, then he stepped up to me closer and embarrassed, and hurriedly told me his sad story: came from Ukraine to Moscow to earn money, hired, he worked, worked for six months, but he was not paid, now he wants to go home, no money for a ticket. "The main thing is to get to Konotop, there are friends..." He asked the chief of the train to take him on any terms - not persuaded. In conclusion: "Do you know who need building work, at least for a day... Maybe, you have some addresses, contacts in Moscow, I would have worked, and would have bought the ticket..." I had no contacts in Moscow. I offered him 100 rubles, he took in his hand the piece of paper, apparently regretting that this is not 3 000 - the amount of the ticket price to Konotop.

I went to the side of my last wagon, but the thought of this man haunted me.... Fumbled in the purse another 200 rubles, returned, searched him by eyes - he was standing on the very edge of the platform, blankly staring down. I touched his sleeve:

- Here's another 200. And ask chiefs - one refused, the other would not refuse, not all bosses are the same...

I moved further. But there was no better.

Train Moscow-Sofia. My neighbor on the coupe blue-eyed Tamila - is going to visit his parents in Ukraine. When I told her about the meeting on the platform, she said that the man was telling the truth, and that it is typical for Moscow, for the capital's employers: hiring, squeeze all the juice out of workers, and mercilessly throw, but the justice is not for them. I thought: I wish I might given him 3000, that way he would with no problems reached their Konotop. I would not be much poorer from this, I would somehow unscrew ... After all, I have intuition, that person needs help.

And sad to think, that the way they did to him in Moscow, goin on everywhere in whole modern world, New York is no exception. My roommate Olesya worked in the kitchen of the New York cafe, where she injured her hand, and almost lost a thumb - she was fired and was not paid for injury. (It's good that not beaten and killed.) Oh, what Olesya... What roommates... I remember: The Hotel On The Blood. Several years ago, at spring of 2007, I went on Spring Street in the direction of the storage chamber, which holds my paintings. On the approach to Varick Street near the high-rise building under construction, was a cordon of police, those their little yellow ribbons which do not allow to go, had to be avoided. Going around, I caught a glimpse of a man sprawled on the ground, or rather, human-cake in a pool of blood. That was a Ukrainian construction worker, who along with his partner were flushed down from the 46th floor by the flow of grout - there, at the last high-level, was not provided even a barrier that would prevent it from flushing... Now this place is high-rise hotel "luxury "- another profitable place of Trump (?) Security guards at the entrance and exit are catching taxis and limousines for all sorts of rich tenants and visitors of New York. Hotel, aka condominium is called "Trump SoHo", the dead construction workers were mentioned then once in the free newspaper «am NEW YORK *» (* Morning New York), and now not mentioned.

...The train goes to south. Tamila came out during the night, and the train carries me farther and farther away, or rather, getting closer and closer to the **S**... So I will wake up in Bulgaria and I will go through the streets of Sofia, where, perhaps he was walking. Of course, it has to be done before, but now - just right. Now, at my age, senses not burning, but afterburning... Smoldering...

Déjà vu. Dream in train: I took, just pulled out of someone's hands a mini-scythe and... woke up. However, that also was not a dream! After all, I had seen the day before, the scythe in the hands of one young Asian guy on Moscow lawn who cut at the root red poppies, and in the dream I just pulled a mini-scythe out of his hands, this way saved red poppies. Awoke: I looked out the window: behind the window wild red poppies! It is so seldom to see, and it's so beautiful...

Soon will enter Romanian customs service... And behind the window are some blue flowers, considering the speed of the train is impossible to recognize. Proleski*? (*Starflowers) Late. For them. Proleski, i.e. Starflowers - spring flowers.

... In the short period of our friendship with **S.** we had decided to have dinner together in his dorm. He grilled meat goulash. I'm a vegetarian, but I ate the goulash in order to please him. At night roommates in my dorm called the ambulance and I was taken to hospital with poisoning. The next day, the nurse said: "Come to the window. Your father came to you." (In the infectious department of the visitors are not allowed.) I went to the window. Under the window stood **S.** – he was taken for my father, probably because of his height 6': he was, of course, older than me, but not in such degree. He stood there, outside the window, with a bouquet of blue Proleski, i.e. Starflowers and smiling with blue eyes also. His shoes were in the clay. Since then blue Starflowers entered the top ten, and even six of my favorite flowers. And red poppies... red poppies... Stop. We stand. Along the way, under the train a dog has passed. It scratched under the train and - next. Perhaps now it will go under our train? Well, it did: climbed and is now on the platform. Near the building of the station sits on a bench a couple: He and She, *cholovik* and *zhinka** (*man and woman–Ukr.), or man and woman, that is, a *muzhik* and a *baba,** (*simple man and simple woman – Rus.) can not be said better. She is a woman that is eating. Dog timidly passed... paused, looked up: "Maybe share a slice?" Baba licked her fingers, and a muzhik stamped his foot, and his face, or rather, erysipelas, has become such a badass! He was going to jump in and beat poor dog; the dog ran away, and the woman said something to the man, it seems, "do not touch", and he remained seated.

That was Ukraine.

...Moved on, again; again, red poppies. And again small blue flowers.

And now – we stand again; after a customs inspection on the Ukrainian side we stand already in Romania: ran two skinny-bitch dogs. Behind them another dog, puppy... Two more, skinny. Flock? Wedding? Family? Here are six dogs run. One stopped and is looking for something. They seem to graze near the trains in the hope of mercy of passing passengers, and others... And yes, there are such: the conductor throws them pieces of bread, they grab and eat - probably, they are vegetarians. Next to the rails, a litter of puppies. The dog runs along paths without fear of anything. These

Romanian dogs - they are like linemen. Yes, kingdom of dogs.

Canine Kingdom, Romania.

...Came Romanian officer, brought to my face my American passport, poked in the record on the first page at the bottom: it turns out, the passport has expired, and I was sent back by the train Sofia-Moscow, what was standing at the station. The conductors of the train, Russian He and She - forbade us to speak with the customs officer in English, he asked them - I translated - "Do you speak Romanian?" They, of course, did not speak Romanian. "Well, then, - he said - I have no choice." He also told me that I have the right to follow back to Moscow for free, it's not my fault... But after the Romanian customs officer, who helped me to sit in the car, gone, the couple demanded $ 140 for travel and taking the 140, just snatched out of my hands, they did not give me any receipt, ie paper confirmations. Rogues! To my request for confirmation of the paper: "Get out from the train and buy a ticket for the next train." But they did not give me my money back. Then, for the rest of the way, they wanted to talk to me, to talk about the "corruption" in contemporary Russia.

I kept silent.

This is Russia.

I arrived in Moscow early in the morning, searched by eyes for a man from Ukraine, who was looking for ways to get out by train to Konotop. No nowhere. Went in the metro... In the approach to the Great Karetny saw a young man named Volodya - on duty in "Godzilla", which was smoking on the corner.

Chickened to see him, to appear on his eyes - it is only the day before we had so warmly said goodbye each other - and I trudged to bypass a small hostel nearby, where I will hang around waiting for a new passport from the American Embassy, as well as books for the Booker Prize and author's copies from the publisher.

Good change: at this hostel I got a place in the women's room and with good roommates - pleasant women. Particularly similar to me were two Portuguese: Benedita and Carina. They were first time in Russia and in a hurry to see everything. Bene from Porto, on vacation. Carina resigned from a prestigious job in Lisbon lawyer, gave away her rented apartment, sent all her belongings to her mother and went on a journey through the world, to know, to understand the world, starting with Russia; will comprehend as long as will let her cash reserves. Bene and Carine soon, namely tomorrow, will go by Siberian train - in other words, it is called the Trans-Siberian Railroad, it seems.... We three, sit in a little room on the floor for lack of table / chairs, and drink dry red wine: a rarity in Moscow shops, that is just dry wine, undiluted. Moldovan drink, dry wine from the shop "Magnolia", we drink, remembering the fun events of the day.

Reincarnation In the morning we wandered the halls of the Tretyakov Gallery. Fedotov; Nesterov... ... ... Savrasov; Vrubel - paintings "Lilac", "Demon Downcast" simply "Demon"...Carina behind, looks back at Vrubel images like taking by eyes with herself on the road. I could not wait to introduce my friends the work of another, my favorite, Borisov-Musatov. We reached finally the canvas with two female figures "The pond" - Bene tugged at my sleeve:

- Oh! How she got there?

- Who?

- Carina!

- Oh!...

Indeed, against the backdrop of reflexive water surface - two beautiful girls in dresses romantic bygone years, and the right profile to audience (in fact, model was Elena, the wife of the artist), was one to one Carina! Carina approached. Became shy seeing this, her own image:

- It is no accident what draws me to Russia...

After Tretyakovka we paid a visit to the "Garage": exhibition of "Museum of All" ended, now there were some Jan Švankmajer, Natalie Yurberg and Hans Berg, and with them - "apology for the absurd, the use of creative techniques of surrealism, interest in the subconscious, the hidden side of human desires". We suddenly realized then that our subconscious, hidden desires... They can be put into words my compatriot from Siberia: "how, f***, do not to drink!"

- For health!

- For the fond memories of the day.

- For the lovely guides in a great past.

("... At home - but as I am in a foreign land...")

- For peace and friendship for all the good!

("...Lists of the dead do not have his name...")

- Girls! Lady! WOMEN! For all of us good trips!

The book is ready. Books are ready. Six copies delivered in time in Booker, and twenty copies with me.

Not ready just a passport.

Wild Strawberries, ie plantation

...Someone has said, and I found confirmation online (!) In the suburban farm Leninskiy have ripe strawberries, hands are needed, ie collectors. Pay by berry.

Hot morning... Bus. Plantation. A boundless field of strawberries. We take by two rows, collect in the basket, group of dark-skinned young people - foreign students that keep records, shouting at us in broken Russian (in other words, with a wild accent). Noon. Heat! I give to my neighbor-girl from right, the headscarf, spare, she thanks, it is easier. A girl on the far left feels not well, sick... pukes. Guys say that finally, it's time, go into the shadows, waiting for the bus to another location, where they will pay for a berry. Waiting for the bus at the curb I picked flowers: bluebells and buttercups. Bus. Payment... Bus. Metro. Hostel. Buttercups and blue bells - into a glass of water; when they revive I'll draw them. Give little of berries to hostel workers, and then take berry to my compatriot: let her cook the jam...

- Help! Help!

I hear from her window. Hurry, ring the doorbell from downstairs... "Eldest" sonny coming out of building, without "hello", goes around the corner of the house, without looking in my direction... gone. I go upstairs and see: her face all with blue bruises, terrible cuts on her neck, blood, blood... The spectacle makes me sob.

- My God! What for??...

- Oh, fuck knows. Choked, then by a knife... Parasite!

- Why, it's... dangerous! Call the police!

- Do not. You know what his work? Fe-Be-es-Paix, or whatever... es... In ORGANs... They brought him a weapon, I told them u-hu, he only lacked of weapons, f...k...

(Proud: Son works in the ORGANS!)

- What's the difference! A man - any - should be responsible for his actions...!

- Do not... Oh, it hurts.

...Bandaging, bandages round, stop the blood...

- Let's at least take away the knife away from his eyes. Fast!

- Well I do not know. Come on... Right now, I put the dough for pancakes for him, he loves pancakes, and...

The suicidal mother's love:

"Love- Mashka-FOOL"

∾

My new passport is ready.

Man and Woman, destined for each other, finally meet in advanced age.

...At morning I visited Alfa Bank, withdrew rubles, for them bought 11 tickets for Metro for 300 rubles (for any case, perhaps returning again, would be returned again), sat in train, going to direction of "Kievskaya", that is Kievsky Vokzal.

When I entered the car, I was struck by a face of man, that... I thought a bit like Uncle Vanya - the husband of my unloving aunt, the Kingdom of Heaven. Some schoolboy stood up, giving me a place. I sat down ("thank you"), and now has been in front of this man. Brown jacket, on his head strange brown hat "meningitka" - well, so tight on the head... Now he took it off, wiped the sweat from his bald head... Warmly dressed, not for the weather. I remember myself in a long black coat, which is now rested in my suitcase. If Man is from the cold lands? - Not from New York - there are not wearing such "meningitka".

Beside him, on the floor - green road backpack. Long legs, black boots... Face, furrowed with wrinkles, which is natural in a certain age... I thought S. seventies, and he may look that way, with wrinkles... I looked at his eyes. Eyes are faded, but they might be blue in the past.... Low brows... Lips... Ch... ears! Ears - they were just such, and only him. Bald head... ears... rang his mobile telephone, he took the phone from somewhere out of his pocket or out of something... Replied in good Russian: "Yes". Then - "I listen". He has already noticed my interest in him and hurried to finish the conversation almost in a whisper. Now, he is looking at me - what he wanted, what he could tell me? His eyes like steel, unkind. I remembered **S.**, as I bothered him once after breaking with my letters, as I was looking for him everywhere, in America it is called «stalking».

... Now he looks straight in my eyes: "What do you need" or something like that... I had the courage to endure his gaze. However, not knowing what to do, did not dare to move, I sat like paralyzed... Iron Man! Iron Man! Iron! This will not allow stick your finger in his ass... even with severe constipation.

"Man on the seat opposite,
Recognize me
Remember me
Remember.

(Lord, have I changed so much, impossible to recognize.

... As bad luck would have, too lazy to wash my hair... such idiot I am.)

I loved you.
You poisoned my life.
You lit up my life..."

Stop, moment, you're beautiful... Awful... But he got up. He got up and left at the stop, before my stop... I took out of the bag (my) book, with back cover up, ie with picture. He went out. I have remembered... I was thinking after, going out on my stop that I could write my email address on the first page and give him my book, what might be normal. He spoke by phone in good Russian, without an accent – hence, he has the practice of Russian...

According to the travel backpack – he does not live here and comes to visit. Whom? What? Business? Good for him, he's from the "EVTF" (faculty of computer technology). He was a stubborn student, moving without sentiments in direction of his goal. Love? On my timid question what he feels to me, he answered, "That would be the summer..." What he intended to do in the summer? Be in love? Woman? How should look a partner of such a man, of Iron Man? I imagined: a tall blonde with a crudely painted face, in a fur coat and scented, perfumed - most likely, the infamous Chanel # 5 - up to the state of public toilets. That's just his voice was a bit squeaky, for some reason I remember another, more courageous. Is not him? Not he.

But suddenly I remembered: and yet his voice was not manly! Damn! He left me on the sidelines of life, and lives currently.

Goose!

He came out, and I have to go on. And what for me that "Kiev", I had to go out of train with him... What if... What if to kick his balls, his eggs? That could be a bright finale! And 50 years, fifty years, half a century of obsession – away. I might remember with smile.

But if it's not him, how could look like my gesture, even more correctly, how could look I myself in his eyes, faded eyes of stranger? Not to mention about the surrounding... For a moment I imagined Svetlana in a similar situation... O, no! No, no, no, no, no. To Svetlana, Lord is gracious. She is beloved! At least, she is married. With love. She is almost normal. Not really: writing poetry. But... it curable. It is curable. With age especially. As myopia... Yet the younger generation is somehow able to survive in the mad twenty-first century. Maybe, her poetry such nice and not depressing, even heals, because her personal life is stable, and she is happy. Apparently, someone in the world has to be happy, to have someone - on the contrary.

And I! ...I was proud that I became an artist: in my letters to him - without answers of course – I said (i.e. wrote) about this. I imagine his bewilderment... Right was my daughter, telling about my creative obsessions: "Who needs it? Hey, you, Seraphine... *"(* Séraphine Louis, or De Senlis - French artist-naivist, 1864-1942)

Maybe it was his double?

99% it was him.

("Is he...")

However, 1% - for a double, and I'll buy a ticket.

... I bought a ticket.

This time, I called my compatriot-Siberian girl-Muscovite, for farewell: because we can not choose our native people. And she came, rushed to see me with a bag with "cucumbers-tomatoes", boiled eggs, jams and even most of those berries, with plantation farm named after Lenin. Listening to her monotonous stories about her grandson Mishenka and "f***d in the mouth" sons (at this point I would like to our conductor did not understand Russian), I saw in front of me not emaciated woman c yellow from smoke teeth-dominoes and knife cuts on the neck - traces of filial care at home, but curly red-haired little girl in a blue dress to the knees standing on the shore of our Siberian river... Golden curls shone in the sun... Suddenly, she asked me:

- You remember, Nina, as you and I wandered on Snake Mountain?

But the conductor demanded "the accompanying to release the wagons," she frantically embraced me, jumped on to the platform... The train started. I remembered...

It was a sunny day in July. We took the buckets and headed for picking wild berry... Waded across the river... We walked along the path, paved by collective farm cattle. Left - stunted trees. On the right, we see: oat field with the blue cornflowers.

We decided to walk-on this field, tearing cornflowers, chopping off the armfuls, not thinking that it is unwise to tear cornflowers at the beginning of the campaign, that cornflowers will soon wither - so it will be... Oats and cornflowers were on level of her cupola, and when I turned around to say "hey, don't lag behind" - I saw a mound of golden curls. We went to the foot of some covered by grass mountain. I said:

- There should be a berry place!

Waving with bouquets and buckets, we ran uphill, and... and were surrounded by snakes. Vipers - each on a hummock - basked on the sun curled, and when we appeared - they dissatisfiedly hissed, pulling up their heads... Clutching our hands, hand-in hand, we flew down and then long raced toward the river, i.e. to our homes, without the road without fruit, without cornflowers, without buckets...

Yeah... Fate has brought us with her... in the "friendly female staff," "personnel féminin amical». But why is she now thought about it?

...My neighbors on the coupe, this time, not counting those who sit down for a couple of stops: the silent widow of Bulgarian, and talkative Russian girl over 40, who dreams of a successful marriage, and currently goes to a tour with some group (all other members of the group in another wagon) in the hope of a fateful meeting. All the way a lot and convincingly she said that there is no love, and that she does not believe in love and does not advise us. She came out at some stop in Romania, this is the group' route. I confessed widow Bulgarians that this mature girl did not convince my, that my trip, mostly due... I told her about **S.** The widow, spoke in reply and had a long talk, she recalled how she met her husband when he came with the builders group into her town to build something; how she was touched by his modesty and his love; as she had to pass through the mother's resistance and break with her groom - for the sake of Bulgarian. How they lived and how he died... The train arrived in Sofia, she had to continue her way to Burgas, where her home and I promised to come to her.

Sofia!

Sofia... In the summer smells of roses. In winter a whiff of birch twigs, as in the Russian baths. All entangled with tram lines, Sofia...

Cracked sidewalks...

South Park on the way to the street Louis Ayer, the former Nikola Kamenov street. I know nothing about one, nor about the other, so do not see the point in renaming. Whatever it was, I found, I had come. Not too comfortable place for professional **S**.: dirty ragged walls of houses, jagged street pavements, potholes - the approaches to the porch. On the way - stray dogs, I turn away without being able to do something for help, the dogs doing the same thing: turn away from me...

So his street now called by another name, namely Louis Ayer. The number of his house I do not remember, remember that begins with "two hundred and fifty..." three? Five? Somehow, it seems ending must be odd. Entrance - either "G", or "D", or some another letter of the alphabet. I have long ceased to write to him, and had forgotten the exact address.

... When I went the first time to look for this street, to his house, a young attendant Hostel Sisi in response to my "I am going to look for my first love" - looked in surprise: "What is the love?" The New Generation lives with other concepts and other ideals. Not counting, of course, poetic natures like Svetlana... Rather, Svetlanas: Bulgarian widow's name too... Svetlana. Although Svetlana II is not so new-generation... Maybe it's because of the first name?* (*Svetlana means in Russian: Shining, Bright.) Have to be careful in the future expressions. Now I go without further ado, every day - Louis Ayer Street. The way is not so short.

I have to cross the tram lines. In domestic literature, ie Bulgarian, there was not one of Misha Berlios, but there was Dorothea, who is able to fly* (* "Barrier" by Pavel Vezhinov), and this skill in Sofia, entangled by tramways, very handy.

And all the way to the Louis Ayer - plum trees, wild plum. And flowers, roses...

When I was going back after the first visit to the Louis Ayer, and walked along the South Park, it started to rain. I saw in the depths of park a low white house what turned out a toilet. A woman in a floral dress in the box office window sold me a ticket for few stotinkas, she said: go to the left, the women's section is to the left. The inside of the toilet was shining purity - would compete in the comfort and cleanliness with the New York toilet in Brian Park, recognized and named the best in the world. Only here in Sofia South Park's restroom, a shortage of Baroque music, which sounds in the interiors Brayan Park, but without the Baroque music in the toilet, one can peacefully to live, that is to...

...Came out of the cabin: there, beyond the threshold, rainy showers. The door of a cash room opened, and woman in a floral dress stood beside me:

- You'd better wait here when the rain will pass...

Her name was Nadka. She studied Russian in school, in university. She worked, she said, "the technical editor for the press, friendly." But after all those changes... Silence... ("I know - I thought. - It's good when you have a house.")

Rain has passed, we said goodbye.

... Every time I cross the tram way with a sinking heart: oh, as if not to lose my head like MischaBerlioz.* (*I remind, "Master and Margarita" by M.Bulgakov) Need to get used to.

Immediately upon arrival to Sofia I found a Russian book store and passed for sale two books, two "things". A week later visited the store - books on a shelf not seen, decided: sold. Already! Hooray. Two young saleswomen not "boom-boom" in Russian language, however, with the help of gestures sent me - directed me to a nearby staircase upstairs to where the books were registered. Here came to me out of some cubby a vicious lady in black, she threw into me my two books. (And I hoped for revenue...)

- Take.

- Zascho *? (*Why? - Bulg.)

- Sign here.

Now, at the bus station... A man will be waiting for me - he will take me and will show the cheapest house for sale, a house that I can buy only after the "Booker" award. This person will be waiting for me in Pleven, but Pleven I have to reach by bus.

From the bus window: Bulgaria, almost like my old dream: a huge abandoned orchard... However, the garden. Field. Fields. Sunflowers and Corn.

Pleven - quiet gray city, apparently, in the past the industrial and festive, but for now just silent and gray. At the bus stop waiting for me a man from the agency Lubomyr, very nice, smiling man. I sit in Lubomyr's car - and further. Lyubomir says fondly of places of history which we pass - that the bridge was built two thousand and something years ago by the Romans, here is the wall... Outside - continuation of fields of blooming sunflowers... green the mountains. Only the lady in the black from the Russian bookstore - invisibly with us... ("Why is she... .. Hey, get out")

The house for sale looks abandoned, its owner somewhere in Italy: this worldwide scattering... Scares a well in the yard, bottomless, almost bottomless, and the need to acquire a kind of "pump"... I imagine my future pets, and they shall be mine, cats and dogs, who are at risk of falling into this horrible pit. I'm ready to "no", but not to this dear man, he was just a driver... The agent is pretty girl; on photo looks like that woman, the sister of **S**. that came in my dream, in a dilapidated house, and even her namesake... Hm... How to say her "no"? Indoors, forgotten in a drawer or just simply thrown away, a photo of a beautiful middle-aged woman with sad, dark eyes. Perhaps the mother, whose son left for Italy, and she died alone... Back to Sofia, in Hostel Mostel... to be ready to tell to my agent, that I can not give consent now. I overspent on Booker, travel, passport, etc.

... On Vitosha Boulevard there is a bookstore, not of Russian books, and the other, biger, big, "Knizharnitsa Helicon." How I had not thought to ask? - I went and asked (although ready in advance to hear their "no") if they can take for sale my books. Premonitions not deceived me: "No". Wandering then on the first floor between the shelves with local authors, I sought and found, stumbled on: "Marco R." Marco! Writer - Bulgarian in Paris! Publisher is also Bulgarian. Here are three of his books, all in Bulgarian, I choose - chose and bought one that is about life in the pre-perestroika Bulgaria. Delving into the text is not without a terrible effort of my brain hemispheres of left and right, I understand that this is the fate of a young man for whom there were so many restrictions, so many restrictions... I will finish reading on my return to... (Where to?) I am wondered: What, if my **S**. in Paris? And they are neighbors with Marco? Maybe, after all this... Quite possible. And in general - "Whom did we love?" I remembered the feeling of a kind of transparent wall between us, that is, between **S**. and me, the walls on which I delicately f*** my forehead ("Oh, sho tse take?"- "What is it- Ukr.), asking him:

"How do you feel about me?"
"That would be the summer..."
"How..."
"That would be the summer..."

~

Again I came to the Louis Ayer. ...Climb the stairs of the porch of the grocery store. Inside... Wander between rows of stale fruit and economic details. Then bought socks. The cashier asked in Bulgarian if I need "Torba"* (*bag). I shook my head "no", it is understood as a gesture of "yes", that is to say "yes" in Bulgarian, she gave plastic bag and deducted half leva. Okay. Now - cafeteria. It is, in fact, the purpose of my voyage: to buy a coffee and something to chew – no matter what to chew, to sit on the veranda and look around from the height of the porch, hoping to see him. I bought coffee and "banitsa" * (* puff pastry with cheese), will soon have heartburn from these "Banica"; sit, watching. Around the house 253 (two hundred and fifty three), and the entrance "D" - the most probable place of his residence - sit two people: an elderly thin man and an elderly woman in a dark blue dress with a dark blue scarf on her head.

Actually, it was possible to see, to read the names on the mailboxes which are at each entrance, however, not all, but... Flying pigeons ate my banitsa. A gust of wind knocked over a paper cup of coffee. Damn you! I got up, went down - and to the couple. Deep breath - and exhale:

- Excuse me. I'm looking for my friend, with whom we studied together... many years ago... ("50...") in Moscow. His name is S....

A woman in a dark blue looked angrily from below from her seat, shook her head:

- Ne znavam * (* I do not know-Bulg.)

The man, however, was more disposed to contact and said in good Russian:

- I, unfortunately, do not live here, so I do not know.

- It's a street Nikola Kamenov? I mean...

- Yes, yes, it is the former Nikola Kamenov streets, yes. Now - Louis Ayer.

- Spasibo. Blagodaria.* (* Thank you - Rus., then Bulg.)

I crept back, in the same way, through the passages, crossing the tram lines and other lines...

~

... I look out the window. I am on another planet, outside - the delta-plans - this is the local transport. Below - a green lawn dotted with white stars blossoming rime. It is nice here. I was taken and brought here. In parting, I remember, UFO with me aboard made orbit around the earth - it took a night. And I remember also, the whole night was rain...

...Woke up at the hostel. Oh, it was a dream... It is a pity.

Tomorrow fly to New York. I will go again on this street, Louis Ayer.

~

February...

I look on the world through a glass window. "What to cook for dinner?" Well. It's only morning, but I thought "what to cook for dinner." Taming? ...Simple potatoes. Cook. Look. Look out the window. Continue to remember.

... Information about the candidates to the winners of the "Booker" I already received online at Sofia Hostel "Mostel". I was not even in the long list. So, I can not see a house in Bulgaria. Well, let. Good that I learned it soon, and now I do not need to suffer expectations for another three months, expectations of a short list, in which I had hoped to be. Suddenly I remembered that when I asked the Beautiful Editor: "Did they read these Jurors of Booker, do they read all (or anything of) what sent to them by the authors?" - She laughed - my question seemed funny, and she replied with a joke: "Rather not." Now, I thought: but in fact, why to read? Why read mine... Maybe even among members of the jury, many share the views and fears of my countrywoman:

It was 7-8 years ago. I arrived in Moscow, called her and we agreed to go together in our Siberian village. I offered to go through Novosibirsk - where to meet, to see a familiar writer, member of the Russian Writers' Club. She did not agree: "For what f***... to see, if that meeting won't be put in the mouth."

I changed my mind to go via Novosibirsk. It is reasonable, according to her, the meeting will not put in the mouth. Let's go via Sverdlovsk, it's shorter. Arrived... We stopped at the house of Katya - our homes for a long time were already not ours.

In the village - across-the drinking, in which my countrywoman, as they say, took active participation.

A week later, I offered Katya's niece – Olya, girl fourteen years, to go by bus to the town of my loveless aunt, and take a shower, if she will allow. The aunt allowed us to take shower, and left us to sleep in her home. In the morning - the bus back. When we left the bus - seen racing towards us the crowd of drunk village citizens, who seized the girl in their arms and wailed with joy: "Oh you Olenka, oh yes you are alive and well, and we were told that Nina brought you to the Novosibirsk *writer*!"

Beauty Editor laughed over the story, then:

- I wonder how they imagine an *editor*?

- Oh, it is terrible to think...

(And there is still such a beast: *poet*...

With regards to the *artist* - so this is definitely from the "evil"*). (*in Russian "artist" – "hudozhnik", "hudo-" means "evil")

∼

... Then I canceled a meeting with the sales agent; she, my agent, wanted to sign a contract, and could not understand why I canceled the meeting.

Once again I visited the bookstore - not Russian bookstore, where Lady in Black humiliated me, but the one where the books by Marco R. All of his books were published with one Bulgarian publishing house and all of them in Bulgarian language. Parisian stories imbued with unctuous admiration Paris. And this is Bulgarian? "At home, as in a foreign land", like mine... I will read after my return. (Where to?)

It's time to say goodbye.

There has already been reserved a plane ticket to New York tomorrow, and I went for the last time on the street, Louis Ayer. Grab a raincoat, maybe it will rain" - Sisi said. And I grabbed the raincoat.... Keys to the hotel - in the pocket.

Again Louis Ayer, again this porch. Again I bought coffee and sat on the porch, threw my raincoat on the chair back.... I sat for a long time, looked at the incoming, outgoing, sitting and passing by. Here is a sad gray-haired man in sunglasses... woman climbs the stairs, with glasses too, dark glasses, and she leads him away. He was not **S**. Here came, sat at a table on the left, three middle-aged men, talking animatedly in Bulgarian language, smoking, drinking beer. No one of them looks like **S**.

...Came out of the shop laden with purchases - a bag in each hand - an old man in sweatpants, gray as a Harrier. Sharply stopped next to me, looked at close range, flashed his blue eyes, just turned abruptly and walked around the corner, somewhere in the bushes, somewhere in the direction of hidden in the bushes homes. Oh. I did not know that there are porch and descent. I sit as a rooted to my metal chair... He! Is he? Catch up? To shout "Stop!"?! If he's gone so sharply, then won't stop. Now somewhere in the kitchen at home, sitting, puts on the table what he bought, unhappy, perhaps ashamed of his own appearance, these half-mast training pants...

Get up. I'm leaving. I do not want to make people on the porch saw my tears... Walking along the deserted South Park, I cry, bitterly, sob. O Lord! I wish to disappear from the world where I so much and so strongly loved... To disappear! It's all I want. Not needed to anyone, broken, forgotten... Revelation: in fact no one has ever loved me, won't remember, won't be sorry. NO ONE, NEVER. It hurts!! To disappear!... Here rose, beautiful wild red rose... From somewhere flew a large blue butterfly; It landed on the rose. I reached my arm out to her, for her, for the blue butterfly. The butterfly disappeared, and red rose plunged a spike in my wrist, and spurted and spurted blood. Stop the bleeding – I try to take a paper napkin from my raincoat pocket, my cloak... There no raincoat.

Remembered, that the cloak was there on the back of a chair, the raincoat, and in addition to the paper napkins - the keys to the hostel. Back! ...looked for how to clamp the wound, stop bleeding, tore a burdock leaf, it did not help. Fountain of blood. Another leaf... I do not remember how overcame the way to the Louis Ayer. Remember only, when I ran through the park, I saw Nadka, she waved to me...

The veranda is empty. I went inside - at the table a group of men, among them a young brunet, apparently the owner.

- Do you speak Russian?

- Yes, why? What with your arm?

- I was here... I left a raincoat. Cloak... Beige... Beige cloak.

- Beige? Cloak? Ah... Yes, yes. (Somewhere in the direction of the shelves:) Hey! Kazhi Tosi old man... a plumber... That is not e otishl in kashti? * (* Hey, tell it... our old man, the plumber... He had not gone home?)

Opened back door, and to me with the cloak over his arm went "old man"...

S-S-S...

- Kakva e stala s rkata? * (* What with your arm?)

- **S**-s- ...

- Kakvo...

- That t... butterfly... rose...

- Kakvo butterfly, kakvo rose? Sprve krveneto, oblechi... Ela pri men! Brdzo!* (*Stop the bleeding, bandage... Come to me! Fast!)

...House 253! Entrance - not one where the old evil woman in dark-blue was sitting, not "D", but to its left, entrance "G".

We talked all night. We had something to tell (and even more things to keep silent - me, and him, for sure), after all half a century has passed.

- Plumber! I thought you were a scientist...

Yes. Imashev mnogo promeni... Tolkova mnogo promeni sluchva! Az sscho misleh, che si... *** (*** Yes. There was a lot of change... So many changes happened, I also thought that you...)

A lot of changes happened. He's a plumber. (Nadka – toilet worker.) And I?...

We were talking, remembering, all night.

All night was rain.

FROM THE AUTHOR: MY REINCARNATIONS

Beauty and the eternity of the human soul - this is what I want to talk to the reader. The most common and most readily I write about women, about women in the modern world, a theme close to me because I'm the woman and I live today. Of course, the characters of my works are symbolic and often cut from a few. However, to create, it is necessary to live the life of each of these characters, including (and especially) the leading character.

I reincarnate. I can not otherwise.

Reincarnation can lead away from self. Then there is needed to come back. By creating a "Manuscript found in the Upper Bay, or: White Horse," I saw the end of

Dove's life journey at the bottom of the Upper Bay, or the bay "Cockerels", the name of this Bay for Indians who lived here before - it's where from she came to Earth.

In fact, the novel is written in the form of diary entries Dove later found in the Upper Bay. After several years of work on writing, on completion of the manuscript, I went into the image of the Dove, and was afraid to repeat her end, afraid of the Upper Bay, ie "Cockerels". And then I ordered 500 postcards - five hundred of my images. It cost $ 100. Having a box of cards, I invited my girlfriend Aviva to take part in the action. We came with a box at "Ferry" - boat station, which is just on the shore of the Upper Gulf of... long waited for the police to turn away... Here we are distracted with something, together with Aviva we rocked the box with my images and thrown into the water of bay. My paper images scattered in all directions, and sailed on the water surface "Cockerels", the police rushed to us, behind us, and we - from the police. Long ran through the back streets of Lower Manhattan, till we were convinced that the chase is no longer...

"Five steps to Resurrection" were conceiving and began even before the "White Horse", but written for a long time after. I wanted to finish the thing, and remind of the usefulness of mercy - mercy to animals, to the world. (I lost much and many because of the merciless)... to instill faith in goodness, in love.

But something bothered. I was like I am not myself. Rereading that time, I drew attention to the phrase: "I do not paint, but only pose." I realized wthat bothers: insufficient reincarnation! All this time I did watercolors, the last six months doing watercolors in shades of green, I called them "green period", but my character does not draw! She generally refers to those who draw with a fair amount of skepticism. I had to postpone the brush, take away from my sight the watercolor paper. Six months later, "Steps" were written, ended.

"The ship of Offended Men"- in general, one can say, of primitive origin. There had to be at least sixteen men sitting at the table and take turns telling about their offense they got from a woman - a kind of "crown of sonnets." (I like to do my stuff in the form of "wreath", where the following part / chapter continues phrase or part / chapter earlier. To weave a wreath, it is necessary to pick up the pieces by color, that is, the power of revelation: correspondence, memories, conversations, and etc. Some people do not like it. But unless we write, or rather, do we write in order to please someone?) I "gained" 16; long arranged them around the table; sketched. Someone was superfluous or uninteresting, then had to "sculpt" a replacement for him... there were many, and I had to live a life of each.... The main heroine I mount respectively of the episode by narrator. (From me there was only an episode of childhood). There had to be not so much a transformation as "revival"... The years passed.

One day, looking at a box of manuscripts, I saw the yellowed, rotted "Ship"' pages... Suggested publish as it is, while the manuscript is still breathing.

"Landing" - a story about a life and events of a woman's life in the last two cycles, ie 24 years - more than any other is close to the autobiographical.

That is, of course, I have "molded", mounted and invented characters and situations, a lot of truth and credibility, but many - of fiction, but in general - it is my destiny, my life with my lessons, my search, my ways. And I endlessly thank the people whom I met; who inspired me and taught something - each in its own way.

Thanks to the bright memory of my girlfriend Inna Badanova - I displayed her poems in the first part: "Darkness", "Blue Tulips" and "Ray"; Svetlana Oleynik, representing a new Russian writing generation of – here her poem "We Were Sitting in The Park; Russian editor Olga Sokolnikova; my family or rather the memory of it...

My thanks to the Earth what accepts all of us.

Anna-Nina Kovalenko